Michael Nickel
Splinter Works

AF222402

Dedicated to Amy

A smile like a secret you are dying to know,

and a soul that feels like coming home

Michael Nickel

Splinter Works

Short stories

Imprint

Bibliographic information of the German National Library: The German National Library lists this publication in the German National Bibliography; detailed bibliographic data can be found on the Internet at http://dnb.dnb.de.

The automated analysis of the work in order to obtain information, in particular about patterns, trends and correlations in accordance with §44b UrhG ("text and data mining") is prohibited.

Proofreading: Michael Nickel
Proofreading: Amy Bewen

Publisher: BoD · Books on Demand GmbH, Überseering 33, 22297 Hamburg, bod@bod.de

Printed by: Libri Plureos GmbH, Friedensallee 273, 22763 Hamburg

ISBN: 978-3-8192-6713-0

Table of contents

I

THE FIRST SPLINTER

Dear reader,

Welcome to Splinter works, my collection of short stories! I am 48 years old and have been working more or less intensively on these stories for the last 30 years. What began as a personal writing project - a kind of diary for my thoughts, feelings and crazy ideas - has developed into a varied and lively collection.

Writing has always been more than just a hobby for me. It has served as therapy, as a source of joy, as a creative outlet for all the different emotions that life brings with it. I have written stories at different stages of my life - sometimes autobiographical, sometimes completely fictional, often with a dash of humor and sometimes a pinch of sarcasm. Each short story is self-contained and invites you to read between the lines - sometimes to smile, sometimes to think. Not all the splinters have made it into this book, I have chosen the ones that still spoke to me in some way even after all this time.

Splinter works reflects the many facets of my life. The title itself symbolizes the diverse "splinters" or fragments of my experiences and ideas that combine to form a larger whole. These collected works have accompanied me through a large part of my life. Originally written just for myself, I would now like to share them with you, the reader. The stories are a colorful mix and offer you the freedom to browse as you please or to enjoy the stories one after the other. Whether you are looking for a short break in between or want to delve deep into a story - you will find something suitable for every mood here.

Although the stories are all different, they have one thing in common: they are a piece of me. Each story reflects a part of my personality and my experiences, creating a multifaceted picture of myself. In Splinter works you will find both humorous anecdotes and thoughtful reflections that invite you to read between the lines and develop your own thoughts.

I hope you find moments in these pages that make you laugh, make you think or simply entertain you. Thank you for embarking on this journey through my fragmented work. Have fun reading and discovering!

Sincerely,
Michael Nickel

THE FIND

The apartment was silent. An unnatural, heavy silence lay over the sparsely furnished rooms, as if they were the interior of a forgotten crypt. Outside, behind gray curtains, the world seemed to have been immersed in a leaden gray for hours, a winter that had been wrapping itself around the city like an invisible hand for days. The room the man was in was sparsely furnished: a narrow wooden table with chipped edges, a single chair with a stained fabric cover, a bookshelf on the wall - crookedly mounted, some boards shakily hung in place. On the shelf were randomly jumbled volumes, loose sheets, notebooks, a few folders. In one corner was a garbage can filled to the brim with crumpled paper. There was no television, no radio, no computer, just a faint glimmer of light from the ceiling lamp, which bathed the scene in a pale, almost morbid light.

The man at the table - let's call him Elias Roth, even if the story might never have revealed his name - sat in front of a stack of papers, handwritten tightly, with margins full of little notes, arrows, exclamation marks, cryptic markings. In his right hand he held a pencil whose lead was about to wear out; his left hand lay flat on the paper as if he wanted to stop it from flying away. His face, sunken, his cheeks hollow, his eyes sunk deep into his skull, betrayed an inner restlessness. He was wearing a crumpled shirt, too big, faded at the elbows, the cuffs frayed. The pants were dark, shapeless and colorless, without a clear cut. He looked like a man who hadn't shaved for days, who barely slept, who concentrated his entire existence on these sheets of paper in front of him.

Outside, somewhere on the road, a brake screeched, then it was quiet again. Elias paid no attention to it. His thoughts revolved around what he was writing here. He was no ordinary writer. The way his pen raced across the paper, the way the letters flowed into each other, the way his breath sometimes faltered, as if he had to put something extraordinary on paper. Perhaps he was a scientist, a researcher, a man who worked on things he shouldn't have touched. Something had crept into his head, something that consumed him, and he was now desperately trying to write it out, to press it into words, formulas, diagrams.

In an adjoining room, as good as empty, stood an old closet with broken hinges, a mattress on the floor, next to it a few empty bottles of stale water. There was an acrid smell of sweat, fear and concentration in the air. The man, Elias, could hear his own breathing in his ears. He put the pen down again, scratching over the paper as if he were confronting the invisible enemy in his head. You could almost see the artery throbbing in his neck.

Hours passed - or was it just minutes? Time in this apartment was strangely stretched, displaced, as if it lay outside the normal world. From time to time, Elias raised his eyes and stared at the wall, at a faint stain in the plaster or at the books on the shelf, as if he could find an answer there. Then he continued: scrawling letters, flowing sentences, fragments of formulas that unfolded over the edge. You could see that he was trying to tame something incomprehensible, something far bigger than this page, bigger than this room, bigger than his ability to understand it.

Over time, his movements became more hectic, more manic. His breathing became faster, his hand more tense. The pen met with resistance, as if the paper itself wanted to refuse to accept this message. He whispered words, barely audible: "No ... that can't ...

impossible ..." Then louder: "Damn it! Why doesn't it fit? Why... why..." He bit his lip until a small bloodstain appeared on the paper. But he kept writing, slipping deeper and deeper into a realization that blazed in his head like a raging fire.

Suddenly he paused. The pen froze. His eyes fell on what he had written. For seconds - or was it minutes? - he did not move. Only his breathing could be heard, shallow and intermittent. Then he dropped the pen, the clatter on the tabletop echoing through the silence. Elias straightened up slowly, the chair creaking as if he was in pain. He stood in front of the table, staring at the pages, at the carefully piled sheets, the notes, the marginal notes. His gaze was blank, almost dead, as of someone who had just written down his own damnation.

He raised a hand and ran his fingers through his hair. Then he walked slowly through the room, purposefully, as if he were looking for something. In a drawer, a chest of drawers or perhaps behind a pile of old newspapers - it wasn't quite clear where - he suddenly pulled out a pair of scissors. Simple household scissors with blunt, worn blades. Not a particularly dangerous object at first glance, but in his hand it looked like a tool of pure madness.

Back at the table, he leaned forward slightly, his breathing now sounding raspy, as if he was wrestling with himself. His eyes wandered back and forth between the manuscript and the scissors. He did not say a word. His hand holding the scissors trembled. Then, almost silently, he pointed the tip of the scissors at his own forearm. You could see how it pressed a little into the skin, how it hesitated. Then a jerk - and the blade went in. Elias' face contorted in silent pain. He pulled the blade out, the first drop of blood falling onto the leaves, deep red and telltale.

But he did not stop. With frightening determination, he stabbed again, this time deeper, in a different place, on his chest, his lower abdomen, as if he wanted to cut a path through himself. His breathing turned into an agonizing gasp. He gasped, moaned, struggled for air. The manuscript in front of him was stained with dark red splashes. A disturbing image: the man who creates - or deciphers - and destroys at the same time, slashing himself open as if his own existence were the last obstacle between knowledge and the world.

After some time, he sank to his knees, his hand still clutched tightly around the handle of the scissors. His vision blurred, his body went limp. He slowly toppled over sideways, barely able to breathe. The pool of blood beneath him grew, flowing towards the table, the legs of the chair, but could no longer make the silent lines on the paper unrecognizable. The words were there, captured in ink and blood. Elias' eyes rolled upwards. With a final, half-gurgling breath, he left this world. The manuscript, his last message, remained behind.

Days passed. In the city, the winter did not fade, but rather became more oppressive. People hurried across wet sidewalks, warming their hands with paper cups, while outside in this dreary, cheap rented apartment a dead man lay at the dining table. The neighbors hadn't heard from him for some time. There was a peculiar smell in the hallway, a musty exhalation, but in houses like this hardly anyone cared about strange odors. The city was full of neglect and ignorance. Perhaps someone had knocked, perhaps the letter carrier had simply slipped his letters under the door.

At some point, after half a dozen days had passed, the knocking on the door became more insistent. It was no longer timid waiting, but a demanding knock. No one answered. The door - locked. Whoever was standing outside did not give up. A firm kick on the rotten wood, then a second. Finally, the door lock broke with an ugly sound. The door swung open and a man in a long, dark coat entered. His face half in shadow, a scar on his cheek, eyes watchful and cool, as if this was not the first time he had seen such scenes.

He looked around. The smell of decay and coagulated blood was in the air. The man didn't make a face, just put one hand over his mouth and breathed shallowly through his nose. In his other hand he held something, perhaps an ID card or a photo. His gaze glanced around the room, lingering on the motionless body on the floor. He walked slowly closer, paying meticulous attention to where he stepped. His coat almost touched the edge of the table as he leaned forward to look at the dead man.

The victim already lay in a state of increasing decomposition, his face waxen, his eyes open, torn open in a final, silent scream. The wounds left by the scissors were clearly visible. The man in the coat pressed his lips together. He knew something like this. He knew that this was no ordinary incident. Too deliberate, too absurd. Someone had discovered something, understood something, written something down - and it had driven him mad.

The man in the coat straightened up, turned to the table and examined the notes, the scattered papers. Some of the sheets were stuck to the table top, caked with dried blood. Others lay on the floor. He took out a handkerchief to carefully lift the pages without destroying any traces. His eyes flitted over the letters, the drawings, the cryptic notes. From time to time he frowned, as if he recognized something he was not comfortable with.

The manuscript consisted of dozens, perhaps hundreds of pages. It contained texts that looked more like excerpts from scientific treatises, peppered with technical terms, mathematical formulas, anatomical sketches, geographical coordinates and references to historical documents. But there were also strange remarks, as if the scribe, in a feverish frenzy, had tried to capture the inexpressible in words.

As the man in the coat read, his face grew paler and paler. The shadows under his eyes deepened, his hand trembled slightly, as if the weight of these words was crushing him. He discovered passages in which Elias had obviously come across something that was beyond his previous imagination. A pattern, a theory, a secret that shook the foundations of what we know.

A soft cracking noise could be heard in the hallway - perhaps a neighbor poking his nose curiously at the door. The man in the coat turned his head, listened for a moment, but said nothing. Then he turned his attention back to the manuscript. The more he read, the clearer it seemed to him that Elias had found out something that could have disastrous consequences in the wrong hands. Or was it something that shouldn't be known at all? His gaze drifted to the corpse, then back to the lines. It was as if the dead man had found the key to a terrible door and pushed it wide open, only to see an abyss behind it, into which he himself finally fell.

The man in the coat finally took out his cell phone. He dialed a number without taking his eyes off the pages. His breathing was now shallow and he tried to keep his composure. When someone picked up on the other end, he said in a clenched voice: "I need a team here now ... He's found it." Then he fell silent. Listened. Nodded. Hung up.

He knew he could no longer stay here alone. This was not a case for any ordinary unit. This had to be handled discreetly. He slid a finger between two pages to mark a particular passage in the manuscript that had particularly shaken him. Then he took a step back and looked at the whole picture. The dead man, the table, the blood, the manuscript. A silent arrangement, like an installation in an obscure gallery of horror.

The heating in the apartment was turned off, the air was damp and cold. It smelled of decay, of something that shouldn't have happened. The man in the coat reached into an inside pocket and pulled out a small notebook in which he scribbled a few key words with a ballpoint pen. He didn't reveal himself, no sound, no hesitation - but you could see that his mind was running at full speed, that he was trying to put the fragments of this discovery into context.

Outside, a neon light buzzed in the hallway. He heard footsteps in the stairwell, perhaps colleagues, perhaps people from his team whom he had informed shortly before. He couldn't be sure. This man didn't seem like a normal investigator. Too calm, too practiced in dealing with the inexplicable. Maybe he was from an agency that even the police didn't know about. Perhaps it was an international network that specialized in keeping such finds under wraps. Much remained in the dark.

But he had not come here to feel pity or to seek justice. He was here because Elias had left something written down, something he didn't want the public to know about. In the margins of some pages, there were columns of numbers whose logic was unrecognizable. In other places, there were cryptic references to long lost cultures or forgotten archives. Elsewhere, there were references to experiments in secret laboratories. An interdisciplinary odyssey through knowledge that was never intended for the masses.

The man stepped up to the bookshelf and ran his fingers over the spines of the books. Nothing special: a few outdated encyclopedias, a novel in a foreign language, a tattered math compendium. He searched for clues, for something Elias had used to come to this realization. A bookmark, a photo, a letter. But nothing like that. It seemed as if the man had packed everything relevant into his manuscript. Or he had never needed to draw on external sources. Perhaps everything had already been in his head.

Back at the table, the man in the coat carefully lifted a blood-soaked sheet of paper. On it was a drawing - a kind of diagram, roughly scribbled, barely recognizable. It seemed to show a geometric arrangement, circles, triangles, crossed by arrows. Next to it was a word that seemed absurd without any further context. The man frowned. These things only made limited sense to him, but he knew who could decipher them. He needed his team - experts in various disciplines who investigated the inexplicable and dragged hidden truths from the depths of secret archives.

A soft knock on the open door. Two figures emerged, also in dark coats, one with a slender figure, the other broad-shouldered. They entered and greeted them wordlessly. The man nodded to them, pointed to the corpse with a curt gesture and then to the manuscript. The other two began their work without a word: they took photographs, made notes, collected documents, put on gloves to carefully wrap the papers in plastic foil. One of them touched an edge of the manuscript, recoiled briefly as if he had cut himself on an invisible edge. He said nothing, but you could feel the tension.

The man in the coat was now standing a little apart, watching his colleagues. He wondered how Elias had obtained this knowledge. Perhaps through experiments, perhaps by chance, perhaps through a clue in an old archive. Either way, the man was ultimately broken. He was not strong enough to carry the burden, and by the time he realized what he had discovered, it was probably too late. The manuscript was like a mirror in which he saw his own end, a fatal window into a world that no one should enter.

The two helpers finally packed up all the documents and sealed them in shockproof containers. The manuscript would be taken to a place where it would disappear behind thick doors, away from prying eyes. The body would be discreetly removed later. There would be an official police report, but only in censored form. There would be murmurings of a tragic suicide, perhaps of psychological problems. The public was not allowed to know what was written in these pages.

The man in the coat made sure that all the clues had been collected. He checked the corners of the room, the drawers, the niches. Then he carefully approached Elias' lifeless body and looked into his dead eyes for a moment. He raised an eyebrow, almost as if to apologize. Maybe he was thinking, "You were too close. You saw something we need to hide from the world. I'm sorry it had to end like this." But he didn't say a word out loud. He knew that dead people don't care about words.

His phone buzzed softly. He pulled it out again and read a short message on the display, which confirmed that the van would arrive in a few minutes. Outside, evening had long since fallen, the streetlights flickered in the dirty light, passers-by hurried past, unsuspecting. The world continued to turn as if nothing had happened.

The two helpers left the room to confer with other members of the team in the corridor. The man in the coat remained alone for a moment, letting his eyes wander over the crime scene once more. He thought about how often he had stood in similar apartments: men and women who had discovered something beyond their understanding. They had all been broken by it. No murderer had to lay a hand on them, no conspiracy had to silence them - their own realization had destroyed them.

He vaguely remembered a similar scene a few years ago, in an attic apartment in another city. There, too, a manuscript, strange formulas, a dead man who had choked on his own screams. He wondered if all these cases would add up to a picture, a kind of mosaic of a truth that his organization - whoever it was - had been hiding from the public for decades. Maybe one day he would understand the full extent of it. Or maybe not.

He stepped to the window and peered down into the street through a narrow gap. There was a black van, inconspicuous, without a license plate. Two men got out and looked around. They would take care of the body in a few moments. The neighbors would hear the rumbling, maybe the voices. But in the end they would know nothing, only have rumors. In this neighborhood, hardly anyone was interested in the background. People had their own problems, their own secrets.

The man in the coat sighed softly before turning around again. He walked back to the table, running a gloved finger over the dried traces of blood as if to pick up one last trace. Then he left the room, closing the door behind him as best he could, even though the lock had been broken. In the hallway, he met his colleagues, who nodded at him. Wordlessly, they set to work. Within a few minutes, this place would be just as empty and barren as it had been before, only one dead body less and one secret more, which now lay in the dark again.

As they left the premises, a heavy echo lingered: the idea that somewhere in those lines was something that could shake the foundations of understanding. Something that questioned the world as they knew it. But the man in the coat knew very well that such things should never be made public. They were too dangerous, too destructive.

In the end, what remained was the memory of a scientist overwhelmed by a realization, of a mysterious find whose nature was to remain hidden, of a shadowy man in a cloak who knew who to turn to in order to keep everything under control. The manuscript that was the cause of this drama would perhaps end up in a safe, deep underground, or in a high-security archive where each page was kept individually under lock and key. Whoever came across it would have to remain silent, just as Elias was now forever silent.

It started to rain outside. Fine drops pattered against the windows. The man in the coat descended the stairs, his team in tow. Down on the street, he folded up the collar of his coat, as if he wanted to protect himself not only from the rain, but also from the eyes of the world. He approached the van, exchanged a few quiet words with the men, who then disappeared wordlessly into the building to collect the body.

Later, as he sat inside another vehicle, he glanced at the cell phone, at the short message he had sent: "He found it." No further details. He would be understood. An encrypted code word would be relayed to the right people, a machine would be set in motion. Not for the first time. And probably not for the last.

The darkness grew, and the lights of the city faded into a blur. Anyone walking past the house where Elias had lived that night would not notice anything out of the ordinary. No blue lights, no barrier tape, no sensational media hype. Just the pale glow of a street lamp, a wet pavement and a few footsteps in the dark. The world would continue to turn as if nothing had happened. And in the archives of a few insiders, the manuscript would lie there quietly, preserved like an ominous treasure whose true nature was to remain a mystery - just as it was always planned.

And so the story ended without anyone ever knowing what Elias had really found out. The pages were written on, the ink dried, the blood encrusted. The knowledge remained a secret, guarded by those who knew of his right to exist, and buried with the man who had not been strong enough to bear what he had experienced. No resolution, no final light into the darkness. Only the flickering afterglow of a terrible insight that had to remain unsaid.

In the end, all that remained was silence. The same silence that had already hung over the apartment at the beginning. But this time it was even heavier, even denser. A void in which a truth once sparkled, which now slept behind closed doors again. The walls would not reveal this secret. It would rot there, in the memories of a few who swore to remain silent.

Somewhere in the distance, a dog howled. The rain continued to patter. And the night ate away the last traces of a revelation that would never have been made.

IN THE SHADOW OF SAGITTARIUS

The day began like so many days in the gray autumn of this forgotten provincial town: with a leaden sky that had been pretending for hours that it was going to cry at any moment, but couldn't manage it. A cool, damp wind blew across the vast fields behind the military base, where something monstrous had happened at dawn. A few geese were circling over the rows of trees, making cawing noises as if they were carrying the news that would make the rounds out into the world. On the deserted training ground, just a few hundred meters behind the barracks buildings, lay a corpse: a female soldier in camouflage uniform, her eyes torn open and a fine hole in her skull.

It was not the first murder that Inspector Claus W. Kropka had seen in his long career, but perhaps it would be one of the last. The old hand looked tired even before he had arrived on the scene. It was said among the younger officers that Kropka had once been an exemplary investigator, sharp-tongued, tenacious, with an unerring instinct for the darkness in people's hearts. But those days were a long time ago. He now dragged himself through the days, poring over old files, drinking more coffee than was good for him and rarely talking about the demons that haunted him at night. No one knew what the "W" in his name stood for, and no one dared to ask him.

That morning, he stood at the edge of the training area and took a drag on his cigarette, even though smoking was officially forbidden here. The base commander, a stocky man with a gray crew cut, stared at him from the side but didn't dare say anything. Kropka took the last puff, flicked the cigarette into the dirt and walked slowly towards the corpse. A couple of military police stood around nervously, trying to look professional. The investigator knelt down next to the body and looked at the dead soldier's pale face. She still had her dog tags around her neck and in her cramped hand she held something shiny. A medallion. Engraved on it was an archer with an arrow pointing into an unknown distance.

"What was her name?" asked Kropka, without taking his eyes off the dead woman. A young lieutenant looked at his documents: "Corporal Karin Strauch, 27 years old. Shooting training, unit for special operations." Kropka nodded silently. The woman had trusted someone, or had stumbled across something she shouldn't have seen. He looked at the bullet hole: a clean hit to the head. Professionalism or luck? He wasn't sure.

The commander began to speak, in a voice that sounded as if he wanted to get rid of the responsibility for everything: "We have no idea who could have done this. The area is vast, with these old earth walls, firing ranges and bunkers from the Second World War everywhere. It's easy to disappear unnoticed here. The soldier was still doing her morning exercise this morning, then she must have gone into this area. We don't know why."

Kropka stood up slowly, knocking the dust off his worn jacket. He wasn't wearing a smart jacket, but an old, worn coat that seemed to come from another era. His hat had seen better days, but it seemed to cling to him like a talisman. His colleagues from the homicide squad avoided his questions about his private life - the rumors surrounding his former work as an undercover investigator were too dark. It was said that he had once done things that now choked him up on quiet nights.

"Do you have any evidence of enemies, internal conflicts, love affairs, disputes over information?" he asked the commander. The man shrugged his shoulders, looking uncomfortable: "Most of the people here are professionals. There are always arguments, but murder? That's something else. We'll give you any list you need. Names, units, stationings. But you have to remember that some things here are strictly confidential. We expect discretion."

Kropka laughed softly, a bitter sound that betrayed no mirth: "Discretion is my middle name, Commander." Then he walked off in the direction of the barracks, while the forensics team began their work behind him. He had to talk to the soldiers, look them in the eyes, listen to them to find out if they were liying or trying to hide something. Sometimes it was so easy: you could read the voice, the facial expressions, the restless fingers. But he had learned that soldiers were a tough lot. They kept their mouths shut, could remain silent like stone walls, especially when they were involved in something they were never allowed to talk about.

The barracks consisted of long, gray buildings surrounded by barbed wire and a cordon of watchtowers. Inside, it smelled of cleaning agents, shoe polish and monotonous menus from the canteen. Kropka had been assigned a small office in the administrative wing: an empty room with a desk, a chair and a telephone, which looked as if it would otherwise be used as a storeroom. He opened a file that the lieutenant had handed him. Names, ranks, specialties. He searched for something that might match the medallion - the archer, a symbol. Was it a coat of arms, a symbol of a secret unit, a personal preference?

While the winds whistled outside, he invited a few soldiers in for a chat. The first was a private called Himmelreich, a lanky lad with nervous eyes. He supposedly knew nothing and was in the dormitory at the time of the crime . The second, a female non-commissioned officer, appeared cool and distant and assured Kropka that Karin Strauch had been popular with everyone, a hard-working soldier, unobtrusive. The inspector didn't believe a word of it. No one was really inconspicuous. Everyone carried a secret.

One by one, more soldiers were summoned: A staff sergeant who liked to drink too much and hang out in the canteen at night, a captain who had big plans and wanted to be transferred sooner rather than later, a simple gunner who worked in the engine room. Most of them had alibis, some didn't. But nothing felt like the spark that ignited them. Kropka felt an inner restlessness rising within him. This murder had been neatly executed. Perhaps too neatly. He was familiar with such cases - military contract work, ricochets or sabotage.

While he was conducting the interviews, one thought never left his mind: the medallion with the archer. He was holding it between his thumb and forefinger when he paused for a moment. The engraving was fine, stylized, showing a figure shooting an arrow at an invisible target. It reminded him of a star sign: Sagittarius. A stupid coincidence? The soldier had been holding it in her hand when she died. Perhaps she had snatched it from the murderer, perhaps it was supposed to be a final clue.

Towards evening, he walked across the barracks yard. The sky was still overcast and the lights from the searchlights made the base look like a backdrop from a bleak war movie. Kropka thought back to earlier times, to other missions he had once carried out. Back then, in that operation that he hadn't even mentioned by name in his dreams for decades. He had had blood on his hands, washed it off in the rain, but the stench still clung to his soul.

A young female soldier approached him, nervous when she saw him holding something in his hand. "Excuse me, Inspector, may I ask what you have there?" Kropka instinctively hid the medallion in his coat pocket: "Just a clue. Do you know this symbol?" The soldier shook her head, but looked as if she knew more. He smiled narrowly: "Look, you don't want anything more to happen, do you? If you know anything, talk to me." But she wriggled out, saying she had to get back to her unit.

In the days that followed, Kropka spoke to dozens of soldiers. He tried to find out about Karin Strauch's past: Where had she been stationed, who had she been in close contact with, were there any particular missions she had been involved in? In the files, he found scant references to missions in forest areas, covert exercises and simulations. Again and again he came across the term "Special Assignment No. 4c", which remained unexplained. Those responsible, stonewalled. The commander acted unaware, others acted unconcerned.

Kropka scratched his chin, feeling his stubble. He slept badly those nights. The base provided him with a sparse room - a small dormitory next to an office. There he tossed and turned on a hard mattress while guards patrolled outside. He remembered a conversation with a former informant, long ago. She had told him that symbols were sometimes used as secret identifiers within units. The archer - could it have something to do with this? A group that called itself "the archers"? Or was it a purely personal piece of jewelry that Strauch wore, perhaps a gift from a lover, a mistress, a friend?

He was looking for soldiers who were trained in sniping. The list was short. There were only a few snipers on the base, and some were currently on detachment. But one was on site: Lieutenant Marcus D. Behring. A man with a cool gaze who seemed strangely absent during the interrogation. Behring was allegedly in the armory at the time of the crime, but no one had seen him there. Kropka memorized the name.

He spoke to Behring again, this time in an empty corridor between equipment rooms. "Karin Strauch is dead. She can no longer tell us what brought her here. But perhaps you know," said Kropka. Behring shrugged his shoulders: "I hardly knew her. I'm sorry." His voice was calm, perhaps too calm. His hands loose, not a twitch on his face. A professional. Kropka turned away without a word. He sensed that the man knew something.

In the canteen, he later met an older sergeant who, over a beer - officially forbidden, but who cared after duty hours - let loose a few words: "Ms. Strauch was once at an exercise in which a secret scenario was played out. There was supposedly a group that called itself 'the archers' internally. I don't know what that means, but there are lots of rumors. Maybe she wanted to spill the beans, maybe she found something that wasn't meant for her eyes."

Kropka made a note of the word "the archers". It matched the medallion. Perhaps a secret cell? A circle of soldiers who had something to hide. He dug deeper into the documents, came across coded clues, reports with redacted passages. The image of the archer appeared again and again. But no one openly admitted to knowing about it.

It was on the third day after the body was found that Kropka decided to follow his intuition. He was a man who normally clung to clues, but in this case so much remained in the dark that he had to let his instincts take over. Something inside him told him that Behring played a key role. He didn't tell anyone about his suspicions, not even his colleague from forensics. He knew there could be leaks. Perhaps the "archers" were more powerful than he suspected.

At night, when the barracks fell into a restless sleep, he watched Behring from a distance. The first lieutenant slipped out of the building, turned behind the training halls and disappeared in the direction of the former rock bunker that lay behind the shooting ranges. This bunker was from the old days, hardly used, gloomy, damp, a place where you didn't want to find anyone. Kropka followed him silently, stepping carefully over damp ground, avoiding the light of the spotlights.

The bunker was a gray monster, half dug into the hill, covered in moss and lichen. It was dark inside, with only weak lamps providing a pale light. Kropka listened: footsteps echoed, a shadow flitted across the walls. He drew his service revolver and held it low, almost hidden in his coat. He didn't know what to expect, but he sensed that he was about to uncover something that was not meant for his eyes.

He found Behring in a rear section of the bunker, near old ammunition boxes. The soldier was standing with his back to him, as if he was waiting for something. Kropka stepped closer, hid behind a concrete pillar and watched. Suddenly he heard footsteps from the other side. Someone else was here. A figure, shrouded in darkness, joined Behring. They spoke quietly, drowned out by a drop falling from the ceiling in a corner of the bunker.

Kropka couldn't understand every word, but he heard snatches: "... had to disappear ... too close ... she had the locket ..." Then an answer in a sharp tone: "... must remove the traces ... the inspector has become aware of us ..." Kropka felt a shiver of cold. He was outnumbered here unarmed? No, he had a weapon, but he was in a bad position against several opponents. But he couldn't wait forever.

He stepped forward, pistol in hand: "Hands up! Freeze, police!" The echo of his voice reverberated through the damp concrete walls. Behring wheeled around, startled. The other figure took a step into the light - a sergeant major whom Kropka had questioned the day before, supposedly a blameless guy. They both looked at him as if he were an intruder who needed to be eliminated.

Behring raised his hands slowly, a sardonic grin on his lips: "I had hoped you would come, Inspector." The sergeant major took half a step back. Kropka was nervous, but he held the gun firmly: "What have you got to do with Karin Strauch ? Why did she have to die?" Behring shrugged his shoulders: "She was in the wrong place, saw something she shouldn't have. This medallion - she stole it as a warning. We're the 'archers', Inspector, and we don't tolerate nosy people."
The inspector was furious: "And what kind of secret society is that? Do you smuggle weapons, do you sell information, do you murder for hire?" Behring didn't answer immediately, instead he laughed quietly and the

sergeant major was transfixed. "That doesn't matter anymore. You're here alone, Kropka. No one knows where you are. And you know too much now."

Kropka took a step back. His past flickered in his mind like an old jamming signal: shady operations, shady deals, blood in the mud of a nameless village. He had once thought he had buried the monster inside him. But now, in this bunker, surrounded by cold concrete and rot, he felt he was back in his old world - a world where loyalties meant silence or death.

With a jerk, Behring grabbed his hip. Kropka shouted, "Don't move!" but it was too late. The man drew a pistol, quick as a viper's bite. The sergeant major darted to the side, distracting Kropka for a moment. He fired a warning shot that smashed into the concrete wall and sent sparks flying. Behring laughed as if it were all a game.

"Do you think you have a chance?" asked Behring, pointing the gun at Kropka. "You're too old for this, too tired, too broken." The inspector was breathing heavily, feeling sweat rolling down the back of his neck. He knew there was no escape. He had no radio contact, no backup. It was his fault that he hadn't told anyone. His instincts told him he had to run or fight, but where to?

The sergeant remained in the shadows, watching. Behring's eyes gleamed in the dim light like those of a predator. Kropka tried to feel the medallion in his pocket as if it would give him strength. "Why the archer?" he asked quietly to stall for time. Behring smiled: "The archer always hits his target. He is patient, he waits until the right moment has come. A symbol of our group, our method. Silent, unerring, silent."

Kropka thought of Karin Strauch, of her distorted face, of the hopeless gesture as she clutched the medallion. She must have been trying to give Kropka a clue. Now he understood: she was trying to tell him who he was dealing with. Sagittarius - a star sign, a symbol, a close-knit community. And now he was facing death himself, alone, surrounded by murderers.

He raised his gun again, but his arm was trembling slightly. Behring noticed this. "Come on, Kropka. Don't act like that. We both know how this is going to end. You're not the first to discover the archers. But you're not going to say anything else either." The inspector didn't answer. His mouth was dry. The words from a distant night echoed in his head: "A man must face his demons." He had always put it off, but now, in these final seconds, he realized the irony.

As Behring approached, the pistol pointed at head height, Kropka asked: "Tell me at least one thing - what is your star sign?" It was a strange question in the face of death, but Kropka was tired, he wanted to understand, wanted to complete the puzzle. Behring raised an eyebrow, his grin widening. He knew he had the upper hand.
"Sagitarrius," he replied, almost with relish, as if tasting the word. Then he pulled the trigger. The bang echoed through the bunker, a thunderclap in the silence. Kropka felt a sharp pain in his chest, felt his legs give way. He wanted to say something, one last word, but he couldn't. He fell to his knees, gasping for breath, the pistol slipped from his hand.

As Kropka sank to the ground, a wave of thoughts flickered through his mind. He saw faces, places, moments when he had crossed the line. He had hoped to find some form of redemption here, perhaps the final triumph to assuage his guilt. Instead, he found a bullet. And how ironic: the murderer, an archer, like the symbol on the medallion. Everything seemed to come together in that one word.

The sergeant major stepped closer, kicking Kropka's weapon as it skittered across the concrete. "What now?" he asked in a low voice, while Kropka listened in a haze of pain and horror as the two murderers planned their next move. They would cover up the incident, make his body disappear or invent a suitable story. The inspector would end up in an anonymous swamp of cover-up, a footnote in the files.

Kropka felt his heartbeat slow down. Out of the corner of his eye, he saw Behring and the master sergeant leave the bunker. They had to make sure that no one noticed them. The inspector remained lying there, alone, in the cold, damp semi-darkness. His thoughts disintegrated into fragments. A final, bitter touch of irony: he, the investigator, killed by a man who bore his star sign like a death sentence. An archer who always hits his target.

Outside, the world would continue to turn. The murder of Karin Strauch would remain unsolved, or disappear into the spheres of military secrecy. Claus W. Kropka, the old hand, the investigator with the dark past, would simply disappear. No one would know what the "W" stood for. The CID would perhaps search for him, then shrug their shoulders and give up. The rain would fall on the bunker while the shooter moved away. A faint echo of footsteps, a whiff of smoke in the air - and then only silence.

The irony lay buried in this silence: The inspector who was searching for the truth only found death, handed to him by a man who named himself after the symbol he himself found as the last clue in the hands of the dead. As if fate had staged a dark play in which Kropka was just another character who was taken out of the game as soon as he had fulfilled his role.

And so the career of an old investigator ended, not with a triumph, but with a bullet hole. The past, which he had never wanted to venture into again, had caught up with him. No fame, no heroic resolution of the case. Just the bland smile of a murderer who would not read his name in the newspapers because there could be no headlines . The Archers would remain hidden, their symbol undiscovered, their star sign in the dark.

As Kropka's heart beat its last beat, a thought crept through his clouded mind: perhaps it was just as pre-destined. Maybe there was no winning against your own demons. Perhaps it was only ever a matter of time before they met someone who drew faster, aimed more precisely and acted more mercilessly. In the end, nothing remained - no last word, no farewell letter, no confession. Only the glow of the archer in the medal-lion, which silently pointed out somewhere in the dead commissioner's coat pocket that a man who sought the truth had failed here.

And outside the bunker: an empty sky, a base where orders were shouted and marching footsteps echoed. The rain began, at last, washing away the traces. The night swallowed up the scene and the CID, who learned of Kropka's disappearance the next morning, would only shake their heads in bewilderment. And so it ended, without a bang, without credits. Just a dead de-tective, a murderer who called himself a marksman and a secret that remained in the shadows.

THE WHISPER BEHIND THE THRESHOLD

He didn't even know why he was strolling down this remote street that night. The asphalt beneath his feet was cracked, puddles glistened in the dull light of a distant street lamp, which pulsed weakly as if it was about to go out at any moment. The city was out there, in the center, where people still bustled, where lights flickered and music spilled from inside to outside. But here, where he was walking, everything was empty. Not a car, not a dog, not even a nocturnal bird call. The darkness shrouded the dilapidated facades of old, disused stores, faded signs clinging to rusty hooks. The silence crackled in his ears, almost painfully, like a vacuum that sucked all life out of the alleyways.

He was wearing a thin coat that was barely warm. His breathing was shallow, almost as if he was afraid of breaking the silence with too deep a breath. He had no destination, no address, no motive. Perhaps he was driven by an inner urge, a restlessness that had dragged him outside to find something he couldn't name. Perhaps he just wanted to escape the feeling that surrounded him in his apartment, an empty, desolate apartment where the ticking of the clock drove him mad. But now, in this dark street, time seemed to stand still.

Then he saw her. A woman. Suddenly she was standing there, in the middle of the street, as if she had stepped out of a shadow that hadn't even existed a moment ago. She was slender, wearing a loose, unusual dress whose fabric shimmered in the faint light. Her hair was dark and long, falling over her shoulders like a flowing, mysterious mass. He stopped, perplexed, almost frightened, because he had been alone until just now. Where had she come from?

The woman raised her head and looked directly at him. Her eyes shone, but not with joy, more as if with wistful realization. There was something in her smile, something that seemed contradictory: on the one hand, it was enchanting, so warm that it sent a shiver down his spine, but on the other, there was an indescribable sadness in it. As if she knew that there was no real tomorrow for either of them. Without saying a word, she moved, almost gliding across the floor, and he saw her dress leave a fleeting trail in the dust.

She turned her head to the side. He followed her gaze and spotted a house at the end of the street. In the dark, it looked like an old pub with a weathered wooden façade. A crooked sign hung above the door, but he couldn't make out the inscription. No light was on inside. The woman approached the door and put her hand on the handle. Before she entered, she turned around once more. Her eyes silently invited him to follow her. Then she disappeared inside.

He didn't know what was driving him. Curiosity? Loneliness? Perhaps it was her gaze that magically attracted him. He had no sensible reason to go after her, but the idea of just letting her get away without finding out more seemed impossible to him. So he put one foot in front of the other, feeling himself plunging deeper into a world he didn't understand with every step. The door to the pub was unlocked. He pushed it open, stepped inside - and fell into another time.

When he entered the house, he was perhaps expecting an empty room, dark corners, stale air, perhaps broken bar stools and dirty glasses. Instead, he found himself in a medieval tavern. The floor was made of rough wooden planks, the walls of stone, soot-blackened torches stuck in holders, providing warm, flickering light. Men and women in coarse clothing, hoods, leather vests, sat at tables and drank from earthen jugs. He heard laughter, but it sounded muffled, as if it came from far away. No one paid any attention to him. It was as if he was a ghost walking through the scene, invisible to everyone.

He blinked, trying to make sense of what he was seeing. Was this a historical play? A strange theme night? But the smell was real: stale beer, smoke, wet wool. He touched a table, felt the rough fibers of the wood. A man in a dark frock walked past him and even bumped him lightly on the shoulder, but without looking at him. He tried to find the woman with the dark hair. She had come in here after all! But he didn't see her in the tavern.

He walked around, wandered between tables, searched in the shadows, but no one seemed to know the woman, no one even seemed to notice his presence. A singer in a corner plucked a lute, her voice soft, unintelligible. He felt his chest tighten in confusion. Then, without thinking further, he pulled the front door open again and stepped outside. He wanted to check whether the world outside was still the same as the one he had been in before.

But when he stepped outside, nothing was as he knew it. The narrow, dark alley with the broken facades had disappeared. Instead, he found himself in a kind of dusky backyard, paved with rough stones and surrounded by high walls reminiscent of a castle. He turned to look at the tavern again, but the door was now part of a stone wall, no shield, no wood, as if he had dreamed the entrance. The woman stood right in front of him, just a step away, so close that he could see her face.

She looked him in the eye and his heart beat faster. He felt her sadness wash over him like a wave. Her hair shone in the flickering light of invisible torches, and her dress moved gently in a breeze he couldn't feel. She opened her mouth as if to say something, but no sound came out. Instead, she stepped closer, lifted her hand and touched his. Her fingers were cool, gentle, but the moment their skin touched, it was as if lightning flashed through his body.

The energy was so strong that it threw him to the ground. He hit the cobblestones hard, groaned and when he raised his head, everything around him had changed. Where there had just been a kind of medieval courtyard, there was now a gigantic castle. It was as if he had stumbled through a veil. He could hear distant music - strange, alien melodies echoing through the wide halls. On the left-hand side, high, winding staircases led upwards, countless steps spiraling like an endless path towards the sky.

He picked himself up, fumbled for his coat and walked, almost in a frenzy, towards the spiral staircase. He didn't know why he climbed the stairs, but the music beckoned and he thought he heard her voice - or was it her laughter? - up there. The air seemed to get lighter with every step, the steps were made of white marble, smooth and cool under the soles of his shoes. He climbed higher and higher until he felt dizzy. He didn't know how long he had been walking.

Once at the top, he found himself on a roof terrace, surrounded by slender, white pillars, with lengths of fabric flapping in the wind between them. A strange, dazzling light filled the room, which was not really a room, but rather an open platform under an empty sky. And there, in the midst of the dancers - or were they just shadows dancing? - there she stood. The woman with the dark hair, her dress now even more magnificent, made of thin, shimmering fabric that looked like moonlight.

She danced. Wild, exuberant, but there was a restlessness in her movements, a power that both attracted and frightened him. He felt her joy, but at the same time this sadness burned like a secret pain that could not be quenched. The music sounded louder now, but he couldn't make out any instruments, just a whisper, a whisper that made him think he was hearing voices from far away, voices from other times and worlds.

She held out her hand to him and silently asked him to dance with her. He hesitated. He was just a simple man walking through a dark street. How had he got here? What kind of place was this? But her eyes left him no choice. He stepped forward and took her hand. This time there was no painful blow, but something inside him melted away, dissolved like ice in hot water.

He turned with her, step by step, the ground beneath his feet seemed to vibrate, the pillars distorted as if they were made of flowing light. He wanted to ask who she was, why she was so sad, but he couldn't speak. He could only dance, let himself be carried away by her movement. Her lips formed silent words, he thought he recognized his name in them, although she had never mentioned it.

The surroundings became brighter with every turn. The light was no longer just a glimmer, it became glaring, almost unbearable. He squeezed his eyes shut, but he didn't want to let them go. He wanted to understand, even if it hurt. She turned faster and faster, the lengths of fabric billowing like sails in a storm, and he tried to keep the rhythm, tried to find more than just this nameless melancholy in her eyes.

The ground swayed beneath him, or was he just imagining it? He wanted to stop, but his feet did not obey. In the background, he thought he could hear distant voices, shouts, perhaps laughter, but everything blurred in a piercingly bright light that became like a glowing mist. The music... Was it still there? Or had he only dreamed it? The woman smiled at him, so gently, so full of unspoken secrets.

Finally, the light became so bright that he could no longer recognize anything. It was as if the white was swallowing up everything, the pillars, the dance, her body, her hair, her face. He didn't want her to disappear, but he felt her fingers slip from his hand, felt the emptiness that was left behind. He tried to call her name - but he didn't know it. A sharp pain pierced his heart, as if he had lost something he had never really possessed.

As he closed his eyes to avoid going blind, he felt a strange warmth on his cheek. Maybe it was her hand, maybe it was a last kiss he was imagining. He wasn't sure. Time and space seemed to be torn apart, he was drifting in this white nothingness, weightless, without a point of reference, like a leaf in an endless, empty sky. He thought back to the dark street, to the dust, to the dull lantern. He thought of the tavern and the strange guests. Of the castle, the stairs, the music. And her eyes.

He tried to imagine what it all meant. An angel, a ghost, an apparition? Had he died and gone to the afterlife? Or was it all just a dream, born of his loneliness, his inner turmoil? Nothing made sense. There were no answers, only questions whose echoes died away in this white room.

The light flooded into his consciousness, burning a-way every outline. He heard a last whisper, as if she was saying his name, softly, gently, full of regret. He tried to say something back, but not a word escaped his lips. His body felt strangely distant, as if he no lon-ger existed in flesh and bone, but only in thoughts and memories that dissolved into the brilliant white.

Slowly, the pressure in his head eased. The music, the footsteps, her touch - everything slipped away from him as if he were waking up from a dream. But an awa-kening without clarity. No place where he found him-self, no body, no sound. Only silence, deep, all-encom-passing silence, in which every one of his questions disappeared like a sinking stone in a bottomless lake.

Maybe, he thought, it had never been real. Maybe he had never gone out of his apartment, never stepped onto this street. Perhaps he had created her, this sad, beautiful woman, in his mind to escape a pain that he himself could not name. Or perhaps she was more than just a dream: a messenger, a being between the worlds who wanted to show him something, something inex-plicable.

But he would never know. There was no sign of a re-solution, no key moment that brought all these images into a logical context. The tavern, the castle, the eerie feeling of another time, the wild dancing on the roof - all of it dissolved into meaninglessness because he couldn't grasp what was behind it. And she, this enig-matic apparition, would remain an unsolved mystery fo-rever.

In this emptiness, in this nothingness, he waited without knowing what for. Perhaps he hoped that she would appear again to explain something to him. But there was no more whispering, no hand reaching out to him. Only the memory remained, and with it a piercing sense of loss. A loss that was all the more painful because he couldn't understand what he had actually lost.

In the end, all that remained was white, so pure, so empty that it no longer even felt like light, but rather like the absence of all colors, all forms, all answers. And in this absolute emptiness he remained, a consciousness without support, trapped in a vacuum of questions.

Would he ever return to his world? Would he ever see the dark road again, feel the asphalt under his feet, hear the distant sound of the city? He did not know. Perhaps this was a place beyond time and space, perhaps the brief contact with her hand had bound him to this unreal state forever.

If only there was a clue, a trail he could follow! But there was nothing. No door, no path, no thought that clung to reality. Only one feeling remained: that whatever he had experienced was not meant for his eyes. That he had caught a glimpse of something, a glimpse into another sphere that had now irrevocably eluded him.

And so his consciousness faded, slowly dissolving into the infinite white. No waking up in his bed, no echo of the dream that he would leave with a racing heartbeat. No clear cut between illusion and reality. Everything ebbed away in a great, soundless silence.

Would she, the dark beauty, continue to dance? Would she take someone else's hand in other worlds? Could she ever lose her smile, overcome her sadness?

He would have liked to know. But that was not his destiny. He was only allowed to be a witness, a guest in a strange dream that he would never understand.

Perhaps his whole life was nothing more than a fleeting flash in a cosmos of countless possibilities, and she was the strange light that briefly shone to lead him to the limits of his sanity. Perhaps this was the fate of all who wander dark streets alone at night: they might tread a path not meant for mortals, and when they do, they are left without answers.

The glaring white swallowed everything, even his last thoughts, until there was no more "I", only a vastness in which even the concept of "vastness" had no meaning. And so he disappeared, like a drop of ink in a milk glass bowl, without a trace, without an echo. A mystery without a solution, a dream without an end.

Somewhere, inaudibly, a soft melody sighed, so delicate that it was more feeling than sound. And then, nothing more. No addendum, no last spark that shed light on the darkness. Not a word of clarification, not a reminiscent whisper, not a liberating cry. Only silence.

In this silence, it ended as it had begun: just like that. No more questions, no more answers, just a static image, an empty promise. The story remained unfinished, a circle that never closed. And so it remained in the space between the worlds, a trail without a destination, a dance without interruption, a night without end.

IN THE SHADOW OF THE ALLEY

The road was narrow, asphalted, but so full of cracks and holes that every step sounded like a soft scratching on an old wound. Above it stretched a sky the color of faded steel, and the wind smelled of cold smoke and wet concrete. A man, let's call him Jonas Renk, strolled along here. He was a journalist, albeit a rather jaded one. His jacket was frayed at the collar, his shoes old and worn. He had no real assignment, no rush, just a vague urge to find something that would get him a story. His editor was breathing down his neck: "We need something new, interesting, strange!" But what was there in this dead area?

The city was the same everywhere: crooked houses, deserted backyards, scattered graffiti on crumbling walls. But in the district behind the old heating plant, a monstrous building block with rusty pipes and steaming chimneys, there were rumors. People talked about strange figures creeping into neglected houses at night. Others spoke of a strange light that sometimes flickered in an empty warehouse. Nothing tangible, more legends, whispered rumors of night shifts, homeless people who had supposedly seen something. Jonas thought: "Maybe I'll find a lead there." He needed a story, something to keep him from sinking into insignificance.

He turned into an alleyway that was so narrow that he could almost believe the walls to the left and right were touching his shoulders. Above, on rusty poles, hung clotheslines, but no laundry. Perhaps no one had been here to hang clothes for ages. An old sign, half broken off, pointed to a store that hadn't been there for a long time. The plaster was crumbling and water was dripping from a cracked pipe somewhere. In the silence, he heard every drop like a pinprick in the flesh of the night.

He had heard that there was a strange house in one of the side streets. There must be something wrong with this place. An old colleague had told him about it at before he disappeared from the newsroom without a sound. Rumor had it that the colleague had simply burned out, gone into hiding and quit his job. But perhaps there was more to it than that. Jonas wanted to find out. Maybe it was all nonsense, but what did he have to lose?

Suddenly he heard footsteps behind him. He turned around, but no one was there. Just a flickering neon light on a broken window. He shook his head and continued on his way. Shortly afterwards, he thought he heard a whisper - or was it the wind whistling through a hole in the wall? He shivered. An old city map had shown him that there should be a dead end at the end of this alley. But when he got there, there was actually a door he hadn't expected. A narrow, wooden door with weathered paint, no number, no sign.

He carefully touched the doorknob. The metal was cool under his fingers. He expected it to be locked, but it gave way. It opened silently, as if it had been freshly oiled. Behind it was a short hallway, poorly lit by a single bare light bulb dangling from the ceiling. He stepped inside, pulling the door shut behind him. A dull smell of damp earth and mustiness greeted him. The floor was made of uneven concrete, and it crunched under his shoes as if there were shards of glass or gravel.

He followed the narrow corridor, which after a few steps revealed a staircase leading downwards. A cellar staircase, tucked under ancient beams that looked as if they would break at any moment. He felt his way down, his hand on the crumbling banister, until he reached the bottom. A spacious cellar room, almost empty, just a few boxes in one corner. No light, just darkness. He pulled out his cell phone and switched on the flashlight. The cone of light flashed across wet walls, black patches of mold, rat droppings. Nothing interesting. But at the back, against the wall, there seemed to be a passageway - a low tunnel, just high enough to walk through, bent over.

Jonas swallowed. What kind of place was this? Who would leave such a strange entrance open? He considered turning back, but curiosity got the better of him. He crawled into the tunnel, a constriction that quickened his heartbeat. The air was stuffy, his breathing sounded too loud in his ears. He felt panic rising, but he forced himself on. After a few meters, the tunnel opened up into a room again - and what he saw made him freeze.

The room was larger than he had expected. Irregularly shaped walls, as if he had entered a natural cave. There were flickering candles burning on ledges. He heard a low hum, like voices coming through walls. But he saw no one. In the middle of the room stood an old chair, a piece of wooden furniture with high backrests. The backrest was strangely carved, with patterns he couldn't quite interpret. Next to it was a table with papers on it, yellowed pages with handwritten symbols that he didn't understand.

Jonas stepped closer. He picked up a sheet of paper and held the cell phone lamp over it. Unknown characters, circles, arrows, ornaments. Perhaps a cult? A sect that met here? He was familiar with such rumors:

hidden circles in deserted areas that performed strange rituals. The idea gave him the creeps. He wanted to take photos to secure evidence. But as he held his cell phone higher, he noticed that the candles weren't dripping wax onto the floor. Instead, it smelled of something he couldn't place, sweet, almost foul.

He heard footsteps. This time for sure. Soft, groping footsteps from somewhere in the darkness. He held his breath, pointed the cone of light in the direction of the sound. Nothing. Just bare stone, damp patches. Then his cell phone light flickered briefly, as if something was interfering with the signal. He rubbed his eyes. Perhaps his fear was playing tricks on him. Nevertheless, he felt like he was being watched.

He decided to leave the room as quickly as possible. He felt uneasy and doubted that he would find a story here that he could safely print. His boss would just shake his head at something like this: strange cellars, strange symbols, no evidence. But Jonas knew he couldn't give up. Maybe there was more. On the other hand, was his safety worth it?

He slowly retreated, crawling back into the tunnel. But suddenly he heard a voice - or was it a whisper? "Why are you here?" He froze, looked around, but there was no one to be seen. His heart was pounding in his throat. He caught himself, shook his head and crawled back towards the cellar. The voice didn't sound threatening, more curious, but that didn't make it any better. He didn't know who or what he had come across here.

Once upstairs, he found a long corridor instead of the stairs. Confused, he walked ahead. Had he lost his way? He was sure that he had only come through one door. But now a narrow corridor led further into the depths of the building. He shone his cell phone in front of him. The walls were now made of brick, red, damp bricks, dripping vines crawling through cracks.

He followed the corridor because there was no other choice, until he came to a crossroads. Three paths, identical, no markings. He cursed softly. Then he heard that whisper again, a polyphonic murmur, as if people were standing behind the walls. He stood still, listened, but couldn't understand anything. It sounded like an endless echo, a viscous wobble of sounds. Then something rattled and he flinched. Was someone there?

Jonas decided to take the middle path. He continued slowly, step by step, his hand clutching his cell phone so tightly that his fingers ached. The ground was now damp, as if he was walking on mossy stones. The cell phone's light was dim and its battery was beginning to flicker - 20% rest. He had to hurry.

After a while, he reached a wooden door. He pressed the handle and it was locked. Next to the door hung a small metal ornament that looked like a medallion. He lifted it and tried to open it, but it was firmly in place. Whispering voices again, louder this time. He thought, "Maybe this is the only way out." He knocked on the door without knowing why. No answer, but the whispering stopped.

There was a sound behind him. Like footsteps on wet stone. He turned around, shone his cell phone back down the corridor. Nothing. But when he turned back to the door, it was ajar. He hadn't heard her. He entered cautiously. A room, bigger and brighter than before. Candles were now actually burning on tall stands here and a massive stone slab stood in the middle, almost like an altar. On the walls hung lengths of cloth, red and black, decorated with symbols he did not recognize.

He felt as if he had walked into a ritual for which he had not been invited. A fleeting fear flashed through him: what if the people who used this place burst in right away? He would not escape. But he was alone. No more footsteps, no more whispers. The room was silent, except for his rapid breathing.

He approached the stone slab. There were objects on it: an ornate knife, a book with a leather cover, some dried plants that gave off rust-colored powder. He swallowed. What kind of place was this? Some kind of cult chamber? He took the book and opened it. The pages were old, handwritten. Drawings of circles, moons, eyes without pupils. Words in a language he didn't understand. He photographed a few pages as far as the light would reach. Maybe someone could decipher it.

Suddenly he heard breathing, very close. He wheeled around, dropped the book. Someone was standing there. A figure in a dark cloak, hood pulled low over his face. He couldn't make out any features. The figure stood motionless, as if it had always been there. His heart pounding in his throat, he raised his hand with his cell phone, but it flickered. "Who... who are you?" he stammered. No answer. Just silence.

The figure slowly raised its hand, pointing at him as if scrutinizing him. Jonas backed away, bumping into the stone slab. He wanted to scream, but his mouth remained dry. He felt trapped. The figure took a step forward, silently. Jonas heard no rustling, no footsteps. He only sensed a frightening presence, as if there was something here that wasn't human.

In his panic, he tore himself away and stormed back to the door. It was locked. He was trapped. When he turned around, the figure had disappeared. The room was empty, except for the candles and the altar. Had he imagined her? He ran to the walls, trying to find a hidden exit. Nothing but cold stone and the lengths of fabric fluttering in the faint breeze.

Then, out of nowhere, the candles went out. Darkness hit his face like a cold rag. Only his cell phone still glowed faintly. He was freezing, his legs were shaking. He had to get out of here, somehow. He felt the walls, found a place where the stone was porous. He pressed, scratched, poked at the joints with the knife he had found on the altar.

Suddenly a point gave way, a stone slipped aside. Behind it was a narrow gap. He squeezed through it. On the other side was a tunnel, this time lower, wetter, almost like an old manhole. He crawled forward on his hands and knees, his heart racing. He heard that whisper again, but now it sounded like it was coming from everywhere and nowhere. He didn't want to think about it. He just wanted to escape.

After what seemed like endless minutes, he came to a barred door. He shook it. It was open! He stepped out, into the open, he thought. But what he saw made him shudder. He was standing in a kind of inner courtyard, surrounded by high walls, the upper edge of which was in darkness. There was no sky to be seen anywhere, only black silhouettes. The ground was made of cobblestones, with weeds growing in the cracks . A streetlight flickered in the distance, but he could see no exit.

He called for help, but his voice only echoed off the walls. No echo of life, no sign of people. He was trapped in a labyrinth of walls and hidden rooms that seemed to exist according to their own rules. He tried to climb the walls, but they were too high, too smooth.

He sat down on the floor, breathing heavily. His cell phone still showed 10% battery. He checked his network. No reception. He scrolled through the photos he had taken, saw the strange symbols, the notes. They made no sense. What if no one believed him, even if he got out of here? He had no story, just nightmares on the display.

As he sat there, he noticed a small door on the other side of the courtyard, half hidden by ivy. He ran to it, pulled the tendrils aside. The door was made of wood, brittle. He kicked it and it gave way. Another musty corridor. He sighed in despair, but what else could he do?

This time the corridor led to a room that looked like an empty store. Dusty shelves, a counter that was broken in the middle. It smelled of old paper. There were scraps of newspaper on the floor, yellowed and barely legible. He picked up a scrap: The date was decades old, the headline blurred. Had he traveled through time? Or was this just an old backstreet store that nobody went into anymore?

He found a door that led out. Sure enough, he came back into an alley. The wind blew in his face and he saw the lights of the city in the distance. He breathed a sigh of relief. Outside at last! But he didn't know the alley. He ran, hastily, trying to get his bearings. The street signs were twisted, the windows boarded up. There was no one on the street, just the faint hum of power lines.

After a while, he reached a main road. There were a few abandoned vans here, covered in graffiti. He didn't know this street. He thought he knew the area. Where had he ended up? He walked towards the lights, hoping to find a familiar place. But the further he went, the more the streets seemed to twist and turn, the more the houses tilted. It was as if the city was changing its face to lead him around by the nose.

He thought of the figure with the hood, of the symbols. Perhaps it was all a gigantic riddle, a mystery to prove to him that there were things that didn't fit into his rational explanations. He was a journalist, a man of words and facts. But there were no facts here, only vague shadows. He wondered if he would ever find his way back. He heard that whisper again, this time from above. He looked up and saw only black window panes. Or were they eyes staring at him? He was overcome by a feeling of being lost, an oppressive loneliness. He quickened his pace, turned corners, followed streets until his legs ached. No familiar signal. No store he knew. The city was empty, silent, a labyrinth of concrete and shadows.

He stopped at an intersection. His cell phone, last stop, was at 2%. He wondered if he could make an emergency call. No network. The battery died. Now he was completely on his own. The streetlights seemed to flicker as if they were trying to rob him of his last shred of orientation. He took a path without thinking, following his instincts. After endless wandering, he saw something that made him shudder: a door, wood-colored, weathered. Just like the one he had entered through hours ago. He stepped closer, felt the knob. It was locked. Above it was a sign that looked familiar to him. A symbol from the book, a circle with an arrow. He didn't understand it. He knocked, but no one answered. A quiet laugh in the distance, or was he imagining it?

He was trapped in a cycle. No matter where he went, he found no explanation, no rescue. Not a soul who could tell him what was happening here. He felt like a pawn in a game whose rules he didn't know. And he knew he wouldn't get any answers. The more he searched, the deeper he would get lost in this labyrinth.

In the end, he leaned against a wall and slumped to the ground. He was exhausted. The night was cold, his breath visible. No more cell phone light, no way out, no helping hand. He thought of his editor, of Michael, to whom he had once wanted to tell a story. But what story would that be? He only had fragments, fleeting images of rooms and symbols, of a silent figure and flickering candles. A mystery that engulfed him without a shred of explanation. He couldn't name it, couldn't understand it.

He closed his eyes and listened to the silence. A distant whisper, a hint of laughter, a hint of crying. He didn't know where he was, what he had seen or whether it was even real. Maybe he had long since gone mad. Maybe it was all just a dream from which he would never wake up. But the night remained silent and the cold bit into his bones. No answer, no escape, just the endless silence of a world that neither wanted him nor released him.

When he opened his eyes again, nothing was different. No morning light, only darkness, only endless puzzles. He was alone, without an explanation. That's how it ended, without him ever realizing what trap he was caught in. No solution, no final chord. Just a mystery that reached deeper than words could ever describe.

UNDER THE SHADOW OF THE CITY

It was still early when Eleanor Johnson walked down the narrow wooden stairs of her small apartment. The smell of stale coffee and coal smoke hung heavy in the air as she pulled her jacket tighter. The streets of Harlem were just beginning to wake up, but for Eleanor the day had long since begun.

Her son, Samuel, was only five, but he already seemed to sense the worries his mother was carrying with her. That morning he had said goodbye to her with a tired smile before she dropped him off at the elderly neighbor's, Mrs. Hazel.

"Mom, when can we have breakfast together?" he had asked, his big brown eyes full of hope. Eleanor had kissed him and quietly promised, "Soon, my darling. Very soon." But she knew that "soon" was an elastic term in her world.

Eleanor worked in a small laundromat on Lenox Avenue. The store was stuffy, noisy, and the work was hard, but it was honest work. She had learned not to pay attention to the stares - the condescending eyes of customers who couldn't ignore her skin color, or the rare but sharp remarks from co-workers who saw her as competition.

"Eleanor!" shouted Mr. Saunders, the owner of the laundromat, an elderly, lanky man whose face was as gray as the walls of his store. "Hurry up with those sheets! Mrs. Carmichael is impatient!"

"Yes, Mr. Saunders," Eleanor replied, taking the steaming sheets from the press. She gritted her teeth and continued working, her hands nimble and precise. "You work like a horse, girl," Betty, one of the other women, said as she stood beside Eleanor. Her voice was friendly, but her tone carried a warning. "What else can I do?" Eleanor replied quietly.

Betty nodded slowly. "Take care of yourself, Eleanor. The world gives nothing around us. And if you fall over, no one will be there to pick you up." Eleanor looked at Betty, but she said nothing. She knew the woman was right, but it didn't change her reality.

After work, Eleanor returned to Samuel, her muscles aching and her mind tired. But when she heard his cheerful call as she stepped through the door, she felt a surge of warmth in her heart. "Mommy!" he called, running towards her. "Hello, my boy," she said as she hugged him. Mrs. Hazel, who was sitting on an old rocking chair, smiled at her. "He was an angel, as always." "Thank you, Mrs. Hazel," Eleanor said, handing the older woman some of her meager wages. "Keep this," Mrs. Hazel said, sliding the money back. "You need it more than I do." Eleanor knew she should protest, but the gratitude was too great for words.

That night, as she and Samuel lay close together in their small bed, Eleanor wondered how long she could go on like this. Harlem was full of life, full of music and hope, but for people like her it was a constant struggle. "Someday," she whispered as Samuel slept beside her, "we'll have something better. One day." The city lights twinkled through the window, and Eleanor closed her eyes, her thoughts a swirling chaos of hope and fear.

The next morning brought rain, drumming on the sloping rooftops of Harlem and turning the streets into a glistening carpet. Eleanor pulled on her thin coat, which barely kept out the cold, and set off for work. Samuel had waved after her, his little fingers pressed against the steamed-up window, while Mrs. Hazel called him to breakfast.

Work at the laundrette was harder than usual that day. The rain had driven many customers indoors, and Mr. Saunders was even more irritable than usual. Eleanor gritted her teeth and carried on working, her hands aching from the countless hours at the press. Around midday, when she was out the side door for a quick breath of air, a man approached her. He was well dressed, with an elegant hat and a coat that cost more than she earned in a year.

"Excuse me, miss," he said, pulling out a business card. "I saw you working in passing. You seem to be busy." Eleanor eyed him suspiciously, her fingers holding the card tentatively. "What do you want?" The man smiled. "I run a small business here in Harlem. We're looking for someone to help us with administration - an honest job, well paid. I thought I'd just ask if you'd be interested." Eleanor was suspicious. Offers like this didn't come without a catch, especially for a black woman in New York. But something about the man seemed sincere, and the card in her hand felt like a possibility she couldn't ignore. "I'll think about it," she said cautiously. The man nodded. "You do that. And if you decide to come by, ask for Mr. Blake."

Back at the laundromat, Eleanor couldn't take her mind off the offer. Betty noticed her absent-mindedness and spoke to her as they folded sheets together. "What's the matter, Eleanor? You look like you've seen a ghost." Eleanor quietly told her about the man and the calling card. Betty listened intently, her hands resting on the fabric. "It sounds too good to be true," Betty finally said. "But sometimes you have to take risks if you want to change things." Eleanor nodded slowly. "I don't have a choice, Betty. Samuel deserves better than I can offer him now."

The next morning, Eleanor plucked up all her courage and followed the address on the map. It led her to a building on 135th Street that was old but well maintained. Inside, she was greeted by a young secretary who led her to an office on the second floor. Mr. Blake, the man who had approached her, was sitting at a desk and looked up as she entered. "Miss Johnson, I'm delighted that you've come."

He explained to her that his company was a small accounting firm that supported local businesses. They were looking for someone to help them with the administration - a simple job, but one that required discipline and accuracy. "That almost sounds too easy," Eleanor said as she eyed him warily. "Sometimes the best things are simple," Blake replied with a smile. "We need someone who is conscientious. And you seem to have just that quality." Eleanor accepted the offer, despite the doubts that still nagged at her. The work was different than she had expected - more structured, less physical, and Mr. Blake kept his word about the pay. But the biggest change was that she had time. Time to spend with Samuel, time to think about what she wanted for her future. But she also knew that in a city like New York, help often didn't come without a price.

While walking through the streets one evening, she paused when she heard a noise behind her. A group of men were laughing quietly, their voices carried by a harsh undertone.

"Beautiful woman," one of them called out. "What are you doing in our neighborhood?"

Eleanor ignored them and quickened her steps, but she knew that the path she was taking would never be easy.

The first few weeks with Mr. Blake flew by. The work was satisfying, Samuel was happy, and for the first time in a long time Eleanor felt that she might have a future. But as was so often the case in Harlem, where light and shade were never far apart, the darker side of this new life began to emerge.

One evening, when Eleanor was working overtime to organize the books for an important client, she noticed something strange. An account that wasn't on the official lists caught her attention. The sums were large - far too large for a small accounting office - and the entries were deliberately vague.

She felt a knot in her stomach as she continued to leaf through the files. Money movements that were untraceable, names she didn't recognize. It was as if she had taken a look behind the façade that made the office appear so respectable.

"Are you all right, Miss Johnson?" asked Mr. Blake, suddenly standing in the doorway.

Eleanor winced and slammed the books shut. "Yes, Mr. Blake. I just wanted to make sure everything was correct."

He scrutinized her for a moment, his smile friendly but his gaze sharp. "That's what I appreciate about you, Eleanor. Your care. But sometimes it's better to just leave things as they are."

She nodded, her throat dry as she put the files back on the shelf.

In the days that followed, Eleanor couldn't stop thinking about the discovery. Work went on, and Mr. Blake treated her as he always did - kindly, professionally. But the words he had said that evening echoed in her mind.

She decided to turn to Betty, who always had a clear view of things.

"You mean your boss might be involved in something?" asked Betty as they sat together in Eleanor's kitchen.

"I don't know," Eleanor said. "But it doesn't feel right."

Betty took a drag on her cigarette and nodded slowly. "Take care of yourself, Eleanor. Men like him don't give you a chance for no reason. And if they feel you know too much, they could become dangerous."

Eleanor's heart tightened. "What do you want me to do?"

"Stay alert," Betty said. "And don't trust anyone too quickly."

A few days later, as Eleanor was walking through the streets with Samuel, she was approached by a man. He was tall and broad-shouldered, wore a plain suit and spoke in a tone that left no room for questions.

"Miss Johnson?" he asked.

She pulled Samuel closer to her. "Yes?"

The man handed her a card. "My name is Detective Langston. I'm working on a case that may involve your employer. Could we have a quick chat?"

Eleanor hesitated, but the look in his eyes was serious. She agreed to meet him later, after she had dropped Samuel off at Mrs. Hazel's.

In a small café, Langston sat down opposite her and spoke quietly. "Your employer, Mr. Blake, is involved in activities that are not entirely legal. He launders money for organizations that are not particularly friendly."

Eleanor felt her throat constrict. "I had nothing to do with it," she said quickly.

"We don't think so either," Langston said reassuringly. "But you work in his office. You might have information that will help us."

"What happens if he finds out I'm talking to you?" she asked.

Langston hesitated. "That's a danger, yes. But you could also help someone in your position - someone who deserves an honest chance."

Eleanor returned home that evening with a heavy heart. The detective's words had planted a seed in her - the possibility of making a difference. But the fear of endangering Samuel held her back.

She lay awake in the darkness of her small room, the soft breathing of her son beside her.

"One day," she whispered to herself, "I will be strong enough to do the right thing."

The days passed and Eleanor felt the tension in her life growing. Every step she took to work, every look Mr. Blake gave her, seemed to weigh heavier. She knew he was a clever man - one who would not tolerate anyone getting in his way.

Detective Langston's words echoed in her head as she found more evidence of her employer's illegal dealings with every file she flipped through. But it wasn't just numbers on a piece of paper - it was the life she had built for Samuel that was at stake.

One afternoon, when Eleanor was alone in the office, she heard the door to the reception hall open. Footsteps approached and her heart began to beat faster. She hastily hid the files she had been looking through and turned to face Mr. Blake.

"Miss Johnson," he said with a smile that didn't quite reach his eyes. "I hope work is going well?"

"Yes, sir," Eleanor replied calmly, but she felt the back of her neck tense.

"Good," he said and stepped closer. "I just wanted to say how much I appreciate your work. It's rare to find someone so loyal and discreet."

Eleanor held his gaze. "Thank you, Mr. Blake. I'll do my best."

He eyed her for a moment before nodding and turning away. But when he closed the door behind him, she knew that he had seen more than she wanted to admit.

That evening, she met Detective Langston again, this time in a deserted park. Darkness surrounded them, and the only light came from a flickering street lamp.

"He knows something," Eleanor said quietly as she rubbed her hands nervously.

"That makes it all the more important that we act," Langston said. "Have you found anything?"

Eleanor hesitated before pulling a small folder out of her bag. "Here. They're records of accounts that aren't on the official lists. I copied them before I put them back."

Langston took the folder and looked through it. "That's good. Very good. That might be enough to bring him down."

"And what about me?" asked Eleanor. "If he finds out I did this, he won't leave me alone."

Langston put a hand on her shoulder. "I promise we'll do everything we can to protect you and your son. But you have to be careful. And you have to stay strong."

The tension continued to grow in the days that followed. Mr. Blake watched Eleanor more closely and she could feel the air in the office getting heavier. But she persevered, each day thinking only of Samuel and his future.

One evening when she was working late, she noticed an envelope on her desk. Inside was a short, handwritten message: **"You cannot serve two masters. Choose wisely. "**
Her heart raced as she hastily slipped the envelope into her pocket.

She knew that the moment of decision was approaching - a moment that would change everything.
When she got home, she found Samuel asleep on the sofa with Mrs. Hazel sitting next to him knitting.
"Are you all right, child?" asked the older woman, looking at her attentively.
Eleanor nodded slowly. "I don't know, Mrs. Hazel. But I hope you do."
She sat down next to Samuel and gently stroked his hair. "Everything I do, I do for him."
"We all know that," Mrs. Hazel said. "And that's what makes you so strong."
Eleanor remained silent as she gazed out into the darkness. Tomorrow would be a new day, and with it the decisions she had to make - for herself and for the future of her son.
The next morning began with a heavy sky that heralded an oppressive heat. Eleanor felt like the air was thicker around her as she walked to work. Mr. Blake's office seemed cooler than she remembered, but the chill didn't come from the air conditioning, but from the looks Blake gave her as she entered.
"Miss Johnson," he said as she sat down at her desk. "Come into my office for a moment, please."

She swallowed hard and followed him. The inside of his office was clean and tidy, but at that moment it seemed like a trap.

"I've received some interesting news," Blake began as he leaned back in his chair and looked at her with piercing eyes.

"Oh?" Eleanor struggled to keep her voice steady.

"Yes," he said, pulling a small envelope out of his desk drawer. "It seems that someone in my office is more curious than they should be."

Eleanor felt her heart race, but she held her gaze. "What do you mean?"

Blake smiled coldly. "I mean that I hope you continue to be loyal. After all, loyalty is the foundation of any good relationship, isn't it?"

"Of course," Eleanor said, even though she knew he didn't believe her.

"Good," he said, his voice cutting. "Then we have nothing to fear."

Eleanor spent the rest of the day in a state of tension and fear. She knew that Blake was suspicious, and it was only a matter of time before he found out what she had done.

That evening, as she left the office, she noticed that someone was following her. The footsteps were quiet, but she knew she was not alone.

She turned into a side alley and stopped, her breath catching as a man stepped out of the shadows. It wasn't Blake, but one of his men - a burly guy with cold eyes.

"Miss Johnson," he said quietly. "The boss wants you to know that he appreciates your work. But he doesn't like secrets."

Eleanor looked at him, her throat dry. "I have no secrets."

The man stepped closer, his smile full of mockery. "I hope so for your sake. It would be a shame if your little boy had to suffer."

That very night, Eleanor called Detective Langston. She told him about the threat and her suspicion that Blake would act soon.

"We need to catch him now," Langston said firmly. "We have enough to arrest him, but we need you to confirm the handover of the files."

"What if he finds out?" asked Eleanor. "What if he does something to me?"

"I promise we won't let that happen," Langston said, but she could hear the uncertainty in his voice.

Eleanor was back in the office the next day, but this time everything was different. Blake was quiet, too quiet, and the looks he gave her were full of suspicion.

In the afternoon, he called her into his office again.

"Miss Johnson," he began as he poured a glass of whiskey. "I appreciate hard work and loyalty, you know that. But I have a feeling someone here isn't being completely honest with me."

Eleanor felt her breath catch. "I don't know what you're talking about."

Blake nodded slowly. "I hope so, Eleanor. Because I have no patience for traitors."

The tension in the air was unbearable when Eleanor returned from his office. She knew that the next step was crucial - and dangerous.

Eleanor prepared herself that night. She put the important documents she had found safely in a bag and took Samuel to Mrs. Hazel.

"Take good care of him," she said as she stroked his hair.

"Mom, where are you going?" he asked, his eyes full of worry.

"I'll be back soon," she said softly and kissed him on the forehead.

She met Langston in a dark back alley. "That's all," she said, handing him the bag.

"You've done a good job," Langston said. "Now we're going to finish this."

But before she could react, she heard the crunch of tires and the click of weapons. Men jumped out of a car, and Blake stepped out from behind them.

"Eleanor," he said with a smile that glowed with anger. "I trusted you."

The air in the narrow side alley was heavy, almost suffocating. The men accompanying Blake stood like statues, their weapons pointed at Eleanor and Langston. Blake himself appeared calm, but his eyes were cold, and his smile carried the edge of a knife.

"I gave you a chance, Eleanor," he said, his voice quiet but unmistakable. "You could have just stayed loyal. Why did you have to ruin everything?"

Eleanor looked at him, her hands trembling slightly, but her voice was firm. "Because what you're doing is wrong. You're using people like me - people who have to fight to even survive. I will no longer be silent."

Blake's smile disappeared, and for a moment time seemed to stand still. "You're brave," he finally said. "But courage is useless if it brings you to your grave."

Langston took a step forward, his gun raised. "It's over, Blake. We have everything we need to put you behind bars. You can give up, or you can do worse."

Blake's men raised their weapons, but Blake raised his hand and held them back. "You think you won, Detective?" he asked, a hint of amusement in his voice. "This is my neighborhood. My town. Do you really think a few files can stop me?"

"We'll find out," Langston said.

For a moment, it felt like the world was on a knife's edge. Eleanor felt her heart racing in her chest as she couldn't take her eyes off Blake.

Then everything happened at once. A shot broke the silence and the alley became chaos. Blake jumped back as his men opened fire. Langston pulled Eleanor behind a dumpster, and the two of them pressed themselves against the cold brick wall as bullets ricocheted around them.

"Stay here!" Langston shouted and returned fire.

Eleanor felt panic rising inside her, but she knew she had to stay strong. For Samuel. For everything she had fought for.

She saw Blake running through the alley, a gun in his hand, pointing it at Langston. Without thinking, Eleanor grabbed a brick lying around and hurled it with all her might.

The stone hit Blake on the shoulder and he stumbled, dropping the gun. Langston seized the moment and rushed forward, overpowering one of the men and shooting another.

The shootout didn't last long. Blake's men quickly realized that they had no chance and fled into the night. Blake himself lay on the ground, his shoulder bleeding and his face contorted in pain.

"It's over, Blake," Langston said as he pointed the gun at him.

"You think so," Blake hissed. "But people like me don't just fall. There'll always be someone else."

"Maybe," Eleanor said, stepping forward. "But today it's you who's falling."

Langston handcuffed Blake while Eleanor took a deep breath. The alley was silent, and the smell of gunpowder still hung in the air.

"That was brave," Langston said as he turned to Eleanor.

"It was necessary," she replied, "but I'm afraid for Samuel. What if they come back?"

"We will protect you," Langston said. "You and your son. And I promise Blake will not return."

The following days were a whirlwind of interviews and witness statements. Blake's network collapsed and the police began to uncover his dealings . Eleanor was hailed as a hero, but the most important thing for her was that she and Samuel were finally safe.

"Mom, can we have breakfast together now?" Samuel asked one morning as they sat at the kitchen table.

Eleanor smiled and kissed him on the forehead. "Yes, my darling. Now we can."

The streets of Harlem were still full of challenges, but Eleanor knew she was stronger than she had ever thought. She had fought, not just for herself, but for her son's future - and won.

And as she gazed into the rising sun, she felt that she had finally found a new beginning.

UNITED IN SEPARATION

The night was still and clear, there was a hint of dampness in the air, as if the city had just held its breath to listen to an unexpected miracle. The shadows of two people glided through narrow alleyways, across empty squares, unable to see each other and yet living only for each other. He, the man, tall and silent, with dark hair that fell into his forehead, was searching for a place that he had never been given a precise description of. She, the woman, delicate and slender, with eyes as deep as the night sky, roamed between walls, on the trail of a scent that only her heart could recognize.

They didn't really know each other or had perhaps touched each other a thousand times in their dreams - it was difficult to draw the line. They both carried a desire within them, an immeasurable love that seemed out of this world. You would have thought they were two people who had once stood side by side in the light of dawn and were now separated by a cruel coincidence. They felt each other like a distant melody whispering behind the walls of old houses, felt the warmth of each other's presence without being able to see the body, hear the voice or touch the hand.

They walked through narrow streets where the shutters had long since been closed. Cobblestones glittered in the light of the occasional lantern. Sometimes he heard a rustling, a whisper, thought he heard footsteps. But when he turned the corner, there was no one there, just a gentle wind moving his hair. She, in turn, paused from time to time because she thought she heard a soft, familiar breath. But when she turned around, all she found was silence.

He stopped in a small passage and listened to the dripping of a broken gutter falling on an old barrel. The sound echoed in his ears like a beat to his restless heart. He closed his eyes and imagined what she looked like - he didn't know her features exactly, but he felt the softness of her cheeks, smelled the light scent that could only belong to her. He raised his hand as if he could touch her fingers in the air, grasp her hand and pull her towards him.

At the same time, not far away, she was leaning against a crumbling wall. A gentle breeze brushed her shoulders and she imagined she could hear his voice on the wind. She didn't know his words, but she knew they were full of tenderness, full of unspoken sentences meant only for her. She closed her eyes and felt his essence so close that it took her breath away. But when she reached out, all she touched was cold stone.

Their paths crossed in strange ways, always around corners, always just past each other. When he entered a small courtyard, she left it on the other side. When she crossed a bridge, he stood on the riverbank below and gazed into the water. They were like two stars coming close together in the night sky, only to drift apart again and again, unable to find a common path.

The moon shone dimly behind a thin wall of clouds. She reached an old fountain in the middle of a deserted market square. Its water did not reflect a clear image, but trembled slightly in the wind. She leaned forward, hoping to catch a trace of him in it, a shadow, a silhouette. But there was only the flicker of a vague glow. She sighed, and this sigh carried its echo out into the alleyways.

He heard this sigh, thought he heard her name in it, a name he had never learned, but which sounded in his head. He followed the sound, walking past closed stores and weathered balconies. He sensed that she was close by, just a bend in the road away. His heart beat faster, his thoughts danced. Maybe this time, maybe now they would finally meet - eye to eye, hand in hand.

When he entered the market square, she had already moved on, as if an invisible thread was forcing her not to stop. He saw the fountain, sensed that she had been there, perhaps only seconds before. The air was still warm from her presence, his heart clenched. He knelt at the edge of the fountain, letting his fingertips glide over the smooth surface of the water. It was as if he was caressing her skin, fleeting, impossibly real and yet so intense.

Meanwhile, she walked along a high fence that surrounded an overgrown garden. Inside there were trees with dead branches, rose bushes with faded blossoms. She sensed that he was very close, like an invisible companion following her steps through the night. Her heart ached with longing. She wanted to see him, wanted to look into his eyes and perhaps find the answers to her innermost questions there. But something stood between them - an invisible wall, a veil that no one could lift.

The night progressed. In another corner of the city, in a quiet side street, a faint scent of jasmine suddenly wafted through the air. It was a scent they both loved without knowing it. He stopped, sucked in the air and smiled, sensing that this scent must be coming from her. She stopped, smiling because she knew he was breathing the same scent. For a moment, they shared the same breath, the same sensation, the same silence, even though they were still apart.

Like two figures in a dream that would never end, they danced through the night. Their paths crossed without touching, their voices fell silent before they reached the other. But the love that smouldered between them was immense, immeasurable. A warmth that was stronger than the cold of the city, a glow, that kept them both alive. And they knew it, even if they could never talk about it.

Hours passed and the sky gently began to take on a pale color. The morning light crept into the alleyways, blurring the shadows. He found himself in a narrow passage leading into a tiny backyard. He stopped in front of a closed door, as if he suspected that something big and wonderful was waiting for him on the other side. He put his hand on the door, felt the grain of the wood, heard his own heart pounding.

At the same time, she was standing on an old stone staircase that led up to a parapet. From there, she could see the roof of the city, the first rays of sunlight caressing the chimneys. She didn't know where else to go, didn't know how to find him, but she didn't want to give up. A strange glimmer of hope sprouted inside her, as if this unfinished search could mean more than a simple meeting ever could.

At that moment, the city seemed to breathe, as if it took pity on the two lovers who were searching so hard for each other and yet never found each other. A bird called softly from a roof, a cat scurried over a wall. He heard the call, she heard the scurrying, and they both faltered. Perhaps, a voice whispered in their hearts, it was not important to really see each other. Perhaps their love was greater in the distance, purer, so great that no touch could ever fulfill it.

Tears welled up in his eyes as he turned away from the door. He didn't know where to go. But this feeling for her burned inside him, a burning star that gave him courage. She was out there , somewhere, and he loved her without ever having met her. It hurt, but there was also something beautiful in it: the thought that they were both part of a secret that no one would understand.

She also felt tears welling up as she looked over the railing, into the empty streets where his shadow never appeared. But she didn't give up. She could literally feel his existence - in the trembling of the leaves, in the shimmering of the air. And as long as he was there, she could hope. Hope that perhaps another time, in another place, the veil would be lifted. Hope that her soul could touch his, even if their bodies remained distant.

The day was dawning, the city was awakening, people would soon fill the streets. But for him and for her, the world remained strangely empty, filled only with the echo of their longing. They slowly moved apart without meaning to, like two stars sent on separate paths by fate.

She turned one last time, as if she could feel his breath on the wind, as if her gaze could coincide with his. He lifted his head, listening into the void, imagining that her gaze would find him, even if her eyes couldn't see him.

And so the night passed, and with it the immediate chance of meeting disappeared. But the love that glowed between them did not die out. It lived on, in an eternal limbo, without fulfillment, but also without final failure. A love too great for the narrow world of touch, too great to ever be fully redeemed.

Without a word, without a kiss, without even once breathing the same air in the same place, they remained in this limbo. And while the city slipped into daylight, their hearts remained connected , pulled by invisible threads, caught up in a mystery that never ended. Without a happy ending, without resolution, a secret that glowed between the streets, quietly, without ever completely fading away.

THE SPLENDOR THAT LEFT HIM

He hadn't necessarily been a bad person, just a disoriented, driven young man who had lost himself in the canyons of this city. His days had been strung together hours of uncertainty, of lukewarm promises he made to himself but never kept. He had caroused in seedy bars, stumbled through dirty back alleys, fleeing from something that surprised even him when it lifted its head: his own demons.

Then he met her. Not by chance, it seemed, but as if the night had taken him by the hand and led him to her feet. She was quiet, inconspicuous, but with an inner strength that you couldn't miss if you looked closely. Her smile was warm, her eyes calm and knowing, as if she carried a secret that could change the world at any moment.

He didn't know why he was revealing himself to her. He only knew that when he lifted his sad head, she listened without judgment. She smiled when he confessed weaknesses, not out of mockery, but out of understanding. She put a hand on his arm as if to say, "I see you, really you." He had never felt anything like it before.

She brought order into his life without saying it out loud. He began to hang out less with the old cronies, drank less, thought more. He left the paths of daylight less often, and when night came, he tried not to smother the ghosts in his head with cheap alcohol. Instead, he remembered her words, her calm, the way she looked into his eyes as if she could see straight into his soul.

He tried to please her - not through mere gestures, but through real change. He wrote her little messages in which he collected hopeful thoughts. He made an effort to curb his arrogance, his irascibility. He learned to be quieter, to listen, to see the world differently: less as a battlefield, more as a place full of possibilities. He knew she knew his demons, those nagging voices in his head that told him he wasn't good enough. And yet she seemed undeterred.

She saved his soul more than once, even if she never called it that. Her voice, her sound, her lingering gaze - all of it pulled him out of the dark corners of his mind where he saw himself as scum. In her presence, he felt more valuable, almost like a man who could do the right thing if he only tried. He wanted to hold on to this state, didn't want to lose this better person she saw in him.

Sometimes they sat together in a small café, where the window panes were faintly reflective and the world outside passed by in dirty gray. He told her about his childhood, about his parents' mistakes, about his inability to ever pull something completely off. She listened, nodded, and her silence alone was enough to show him that she understood him. He felt light, almost floating.

But the city was not friendly. It had its own plans, made its rounds, devoured destinies, spat them out again. He noticed how the threads that bound him to her were thin, perhaps too thin. He tried to tighten them, spent more time with her, tried to show her again and again that he was willing to change in order to be the man she deserved.

She remained calm, warm, but there was a shadow in her eyes that he couldn't interpret. He wanted to know what she was thinking, how she saw him. But she rarely talked about it. He only sensed that she lived on, continued to radiate, even when he wasn't there. Her energy was not dependent on him, she had her own source of power, the origin of which remained hidden from him.

One evening, he asked her what she wanted for her future. She smiled vaguely, turning her head to the side as if she was listening to a melody he couldn't hear. "I don't want my light to go out," she said softly. "I want to be a star for someone who is looking for the way." He nodded, sure that she meant him. Sure that he was that person who needed her light.

But time passed and she met another man. He didn't know who he was, only that one afternoon she sat with him on an old park bench. He watched her from a distance, saw how she laughed, how she smiled, and recognized the same sparkle in her eyes that she once had for him. Something inside him tightened.

He had tried to be a better person - not just for her, but mainly because of her. She had tamed his demons, but now that he was standing there, half a street away, and she was sitting next to someone else, the ghosts inside him flared up. He didn't want to fall back into old patterns, didn't want to let jealousy or bitterness eat away at him. But the insecurity was eating away at him.

From that day on, she seemed more distant to him. She remained friendly, she did not avoid him, but she no longer shone so exclusively for him. She had found a new center, another man, to whom she now gave this quiet magic that he had so desperately needed. He told himself that this was her right, that he could not dispose of her. But it still hurt.

The city seemed darker to him again. He tried to remember the lessons she had unconsciously taught him: patience, kindness, letting go. But his hands trembled when he thought that all his efforts could have been in vain. He had changed, had learned to breathe more slowly, to see more clearly. But now, without her hand to guide him, he asked himself: What for?

He met her several more times, in fleeting moments, at the market, in a bookshop, on a street corner. She smiled at him as if everything was fine. But he saw how her gaze kept wandering to the man who was now at her side. A man who probably had the security he had never had. A man without demons, or at least with enough strength to tame them himself.

He tried to stay strong, didn't want to go back to his old life. He remembered her words, her quiet looks. She had made him a better person, and if he was honest, he couldn't take that back. He didn't want to go back to the muck, to the old mire of self-hatred. Her strength was still there, in his chest like a spark that wouldn't burn out.

But it hurt. Every night, as he stared at the ceiling of his modest apartment, he heard his heart pounding and wondered if he had ever had the chance to be her star. He remembered her smile, how she had helped him to sort out the chaos in his soul. Now she was the shining point in the dark firmament for someone else, and he stood in the darkness, alone with his thoughts.

There was no easy answer, no consolation, no hand to hold out the truth. The world kept turning, and she was not part of his future - at least not in the way he had hoped. He had to realize that some paths only touch briefly to initiate change, but then drift apart.

In the end, a mystery remained. Why had she come into his life to save him, only to move on? Why had he had this experience if she wasn't his, if her light now shone for someone else? He would find no answers, no certainty to ease his pain.

One chilly night, he stood on a street corner with his hands in his pockets. A distant lantern flickered. He thought of her words, of her soft smile. He stood there, a better man than before, but without her. The demons inside him slept lightly, not defeated, but stunned by her former closeness. He stared into the darkness, hoping for a sign, but none came.

So he remained trapped in his new identity: a man who had learned to be a better person, but without the star that had led him there. Her light, her radiance, now shone in someone else's eyes. No happy ending, no crystal-clear realization. Just a silent, painful mystery in which he now had to live, alone with the lessons she had left him.

WHY SNOOPY WANTED TO KILL ME

The woman, let's call her Elena, was young and full of life. Her laughter sounded like soft bells as she walked through the train compartments or waited at airport counters. She wore colorful scarves around her neck, loved to be spontaneous and felt a flow in her veins that she herself described as curiosity about the world. No one who met her would ever have thought that her life would derail so strangely.

On her travels, which took her through cities and countries she had never been to before, she always carried a stuffed animal with her - a Snoopy. It wasn't just any Snoopy, but an old, slightly disheveled plush dog that she had received from her mother as a child. The fabric on one ear was worn, a seam on the paw a little loose. But for Elena, Snoopy was something of a talisman. He reminded her of a smile, of something warm from the past, of innocence.

On a gray morning, she boarded a train that took her across a foreign country whose language she did not speak. Behind the windows, threads of rain sloshed against the glass, streets blurred into gray patches. She was full of anticipation, didn't know exactly where this journey would take her, but she wanted to arrive where chance had led her.

The compartment she shared with two strange men smelled of cold smoke. The men gave her a cursory nod and then silently read newspapers whose characters she couldn't interpret. Elena pulled Snoopy out of her bag, smiled at him as if he were an old friend and quietly told him about her plans. It was a strange habit, but she had been doing it for as long as she could remember.

That night, as the train passed over a remote section of track, Elena woke up. The moon looked at her through the train window - pale, silent. She thought she heard a scratching sound, as if someone was scraping the wooden wall of the compartment with a blunt knife. The men were asleep, the compartment was dark except for the dim light of an outside lamp flickering on a passing platform.

She looked around and felt an inexplicable pressure in her chest. There was Snoopy, in her seat next to her. His shadow fell strangely distorted on the backrest. For a moment, she thought his beady little eyes shone un-naturally in the pale light. She shook her head. A stuffed animal. Unmoving. A silent companion. Nothing more.

But when she woke up the next morning, Snoopy was no longer lying where she had put him. He was squatting on the overhead luggage rack, as if someone had put him there. The two men smiled at her strangely as she left the compartment. Had she put him there herself ? She couldn't remember. Perhaps just a harm-less prank by her fellow passengers?

She left the train in the next town. A rain-soaked plat-form, suitcase wheels rattling, a mumbled loudspeaker calling out names that meant nothing to her. She sen-sed that something was wrong. When exactly had this feeling crept in that Snoopy was... watching her?

She let it go. Looked for a small hotel, checked in, put her travel bag on the bed. Put Snoopy next to it. Al-most jokingly, she said: "Stay here, my friend. I need a shower." A hint of fear crept into her voice. Why was she talking to him like that? He was just cloth and stuf-fing, a silent witness to her ways.

But when she came out of the bathroom, Snoopy was gone. She found him on the windowsill, half-slipped behind the curtain, as if he had tried to climb out. She grinned nervously. Of course, she had probably put him there herself. She needed to calm down, enough imagination, Elena! It was just her head going crazy - new places, new faces, that was all.

On her onward journey, this time on a bus, it happened again: she was dozing with Snoopy in her arms, woke up and he was sitting in another seat. The other passengers acted as if they didn't notice. Some looked at her as if she was the odd one out. Every time she tried to speak to someone, they avoided her. As if there was something about her that made them uncomfortable.

Somewhere deep inside her was the absurd idea that Snoopy was moving himself, that he had a will of his own. A will that was not friendly. She remembered a dream she had had as a child: Snoopy grabbing her by the hands and laughing, a dark, impossible laugh. She woke up screaming, but her mother had calmed her down. "Just a dream, Elena, just a dream."

Days passed, and with every change of location it became stranger. In a hostel, she found Snoopy with his little arm stretched out towards the door, as if showing her the way out. On a ferry across a murky lake, she thought his paw slipped an inch when she looked away for a moment. And always that feeling in the night, as if something were standing by her bed, silent, waiting.

She became cautious. She began to lock Snoopy in a suitcase, but when she woke up the next morning, he was lying next to her again. Once she dared to put him in the luggage compartment at the back of the bus.

When she went to get her bag, he was gone, and later she discovered him under her seat, as if he had crawled there.

Elena was at a loss and her former zest for life began to crack. She lost her appetite, slept badly, avoided conversations. She was a woman who had once seen every day as a new adventure, and now she was afraid of her own stuffed animal, as if it were a living creature with dark intentions.

One windy night, she stayed in a run-down inn. The guests were taciturn, the food tasted bland. She locked the door to her room, laid Snoopy on a chair and stared at him for a long time. "What do you want from me?" she whispered, as if expecting an answer. The ticking of the clock was her only answer.

She slept fitfully. In the night, she thought she heard footsteps, light, clumsy footsteps, as if soft paws were dragging across wooden floorboards. She wanted to open her eyes, but her eyelids were heavy. A pressure weighed on her chest. She felt a weight on her, as if something was trying to strangle her. She struggled for breath, heard a soundless giggle in her head, or was it just the wind in the fireplace?

She jerked up, drenched in sweat. The room was empty, the door locked. Snoopy sat motionless in the chair as usual. But she felt a spasm in her lungs, as if someone had really tried to kill her, as if she had been fighting for her life for a moment. She vowed not to play the game any longer.

The next day, she took a train back to where her journey had begun. She wanted to go home. Maybe she would leave Snoopy there, in a place where he could do no harm. She was sure it was madness to think like that, but fear made her thoughts confused. The light flickered in the twilight of the compartment. She squeezed Snoopy tightly under her arm so he couldn't move. As if he had a power of his own that wanted to kill her, to extinguish her soul life.

She reached her hometown at night. The streets were empty, lanterns cast yellow spots on wet cobblestones. She went to the riverbank, stood on an old bridge, looked into the dark waters. She wanted to get rid of Snoopy, throw him into the black water. But when she held him in her hand, she hesitated. He had been her talisman, her support. Had she gone mad?

No end, no solution. She was tired, couldn't part with him and couldn't keep him. A young woman, once so full of life, now trapped in an absurd fear of something no human would understand. The rain began to fall, soft drops on her hair, on Snoopy's head. She placed him on the bridge railing, looked at him as if he were a living being. But he remained silent, mute and rigid. Nothing became clear, no secret was revealed.

She stood there until dawn, unable to make a decision. She didn't know whether it was her imagination or whether there really was something sinister lurking in this stuffed animal. Her gaze wandered to the awakening sky, but it gave no answer. In the end, she would move on with Snoopy again, without understanding why she thought he wanted to kill her. Perhaps just a fever dream, a mental imbalance triggered by too many strange places.

The truth remained a mystery, locked between threads and absorbent cotton inside the stuffed animal, between the shadows of the places she had visited. No resolution, no consolation. She was a woman who wanted to conquer the world, and now she stood trembling on a bridge, unable to let go of or confide in this silent companion.

The day dawned, people walked past without paying any attention to her. She picked Snoopy up again, hugged him tightly as if he were both a lifeline and a threat. And so their journey ended, not in clarity, but in an eternal question mark. She would never know why Snoopy wanted to kill her - if he wanted to at all. She had to live with it, and whether she could ever be happy again remained unclear.

No happy ending, no certainty. Just the silent streets, a faint whisper of wind and the oppressive thought that this fear would never completely go away. The world kept spinning as she ran off with Snoopy under her arm, into some future that promised no answers.

THE PATH BETWEEN THE SHADOWS

Her name was Branwen, or so she was told, though she could barely remember her parents' voices. It was as if her name came whispered from the windswept hills that once surrounded her tribe. But now she was alone, a Celtic girl, petite in stature but with taut muscles beneath the furs she wore. Her hair was disheveled, matted with earth and leaves, and her feet ached on the stony ground.

Their tribe was gone. Disappeared in a night of smoke and screams. She remembered blazing flames, the smell of burning wood and flesh, muffled shouts in a strange tongue. Then she had woken up, alone among overturned baskets and broken shields. No familiar faces, only silence, ashes and wind.

She didn't know where she was, only that her home lay to the north behind mountains and moors. So she ran, a bow and a few arrows slung around her shoulder, a knife at her belt. She knew the signs of the wilderness: the rustling of the undergrowth, the movement of the sun. But here, in this strange land, the rules seemed to change. The sun slid hastily across the sky, the shadows became strange, growing at unfamiliar angles.

Sometimes she heard voices. Soft, hissing sounds that crept into her ears when she sat down in a hollow to eat something dry or sip water from a puddle. They were not the voices of her tribe. They sounded like the whispering of crows or the crunching of bones. Branwen shook her head then, trying to ignore the words, but they echoed in her skull, demanding attention.

She was still young, not even the age of those who were considered adults in the tribe. And yet she had learned to listen to her instincts. As she crept through a barren ravine, surrounded by craggy rocks, she noticed footprints that didn't look human. Claw-like, pressed deep into the muddy ground. She tightened her grip on her bow and crept on, always looking for a safe path.

The wind carried strange smells: rot, old blood, moss sticking to dead wood. The voices in her head grew louder, playing with her mind. She heard her mother whisper: "Branwen, why aren't you with us?" Then another, unfamiliar voice laughed, and she felt a chill creep up the back of her neck. She wanted to call out, wanted to scream, but she knew that noise could lure enemies, creatures that dwelled in this land.

She had to reach the river she was told, sparsely by the old men: "Follow the big water to the north until you see the mossy stones." But she didn't know how far it was. The days blurred. Hunger gnawed at her guts, and she had to nibble on dark mushrooms and bitter bark to keep from collapsing. Sometimes she shot a hare or a bird, but prey was rare in this inhospitable region.

At night, the stars lay like frozen tears in the sky. Branwen crouched under shaggy bushes, pressing her fists to her ears to stifle the voices, to drive the images from her mind. There she saw her father, impaled on a spear, or her brother lying in a pit, mute. She wasn't sure if these images were true or if they were created by something dark inside her.

Once she found traces of people: Bony remains of a campfire, an old strip of leather, perhaps a strap. She wanted to call out, beg for help. But the voices laughed at her: "They won't want you. You don't belong anywhere." She gritted her teeth, fighting the dizziness that overcame her. Exhausted, she sank to her knees, dug in the earth and found only worms and cold stones.

When she finally reached a stream, she drank greedily. The water was bitter and stained, but it was wet. She saw her reflection in it: a young face, marked by dirt and exhaustion. And behind her, she thought, stood a figure with a hollow look. When she turned around, there was no one there. Just a bare tree with gnarled branches that looked like bony fingers.

She made her way further north, over boggy ground that sucked at her legs with every step. She fell several times, scratching her arms and legs. The voices began to sing songs, sad melodies that reminded her of long-gone festivals in the tribe. But these memories were like shattering pieces of glass in her heart.

One windy morning, as a pale light settled over the distant range of hills, she recognized a boulder that the old people had described: a stone figure that looked like a bent raven. There, she knew, she was closer to home. But the land between here and her village was deadly. She had to walk through fields of fog, past caves where darkness dwelled.

Every step was harder for her. Her body was drained, her mind torn apart. The voices in her head were now arguing with each other: some whispered encouragement, others mocked her. She tried to remember her grandmother's voice, who once said: "We are part of the earth, and it will not let us fall." But was she really part of this land, or just a foreign body?

The days lost their contours. Fog surrounded her like a grey veil in which she could no longer recognize any direction. Her bow was useless, the arrows worn out.

She ate what she could find: bitter berries, strips of bark covered in lichen. Her stomach cramped, her head ached. Again and again she stumbled, fell, struggled to get up.

She thought of her tribe. The faces she missed. Had any of them survived? Were they still there, where the mud and wood huts once stood? She didn't know. The voices said there was no longer a home, only ruins. Or they said everyone had forgotten them. She couldn't tell which words were real.

Despair slowly crept into her bones. But she walked on, obedient to an inner necessity that she herself did not understand. Sometimes she thought she heard footsteps behind her, or figures in the distance watching her. But when she approached, there was nothing but thorny bushes or empty fields.

The air grew colder, the wind bit into her face. She wrapped herself tighter in her furs, heard her own heart pumping like a tired drum. When she fell asleep, she dreamed of her village, of a fire circle where songs were sung. She woke up with tears evaporating in the harsh light of a cloudy morning.

At some point, she reached a stretch of land that seemed vaguely familiar: rolling hills, dead tree stumps that she thought she had seen before, back when she was foraging for mushrooms with the hunters from her tribe. She wanted to believe she was close, only a few days away. But the earth was silent.

One foot in front of the other, voices in her head, tumbling over each other. She had no strength left to shout against them. She let them be, as if they were a choir accompanying her steps. The world was indifferent, every root, every stone equally cruel. But she continued on her way, stumbled, fell, got up, further and further.

The sky burned with dark colors as she climbed a mountain ridge. Behind it lay the land she knew as home - so said a faint memory in her heart. She didn't know what she would find there. Perhaps ruins, perhaps an empty piece of earth where her people once lived. Or perhaps familiar faces that embraced her.

But she had no answers, only doubt and exhaustion. She walked down the hill, staggered, heard the voices again. They were silent now, just whispering, and she could no longer understand anything. The landscape in front of her remained hazy, as if a thin fog had immersed everything in a milky gray.

She was approaching her destination, or what she thought it was. No salvation in sight, no clear path, no clear boundary between what was and what should be. Just her tired feet on unfamiliar ground, her heart full of uncertainty, the voices that whispered now and then, and the endless expanse in which she was trapped.

BETWEEN CROOKED NOTES AND SOAP BUBBLES

It was a normal Thursday afternoon in this snore-inducing small town, where nothing happened except the occasional half-hearted fire festival or the popping up of a new burger chain that nobody needed anyway. Our hero of the story - let's call him Ben - sat on his crooked swivel chair at the desk in his room. A little too skinny, a little too tall, hair that refused to part in a cool parting and clothes that definitely wouldn't end up on the cover of a hipster magazine.

Ben was 16 and felt like a lucky loser, which means something like: He hadn't really got much on the ball, but at least he hadn't completely driven anything up the wall. He was so in the middle of everything. Average grades, average looks, average existence. His only bright spot: He played the guitar. Well, more bad than good, but at least better than Jochen from the parallel class, whose chords sounded more like a guitar maker's torture chamber.

Ben had a band - well, more or less a band. "The Cracked Strings" was the name of the chaotic troupe. By "band" here we mean a ragtag group of teenagers who strummed around on second-hand instruments in the basement of Paul's parents' house. Paul pushed himself through as a drummer, but made more noise than rhythm, Lisa tried her hand at keyboard sounds, which sometimes sounded like a broken Gameboy, sometimes like a noisy vacuum cleaner. And Ben strummed shyly but devotedly on his guitar. If you halved the volume of the garage bands from the 90s and added a few stumbling teenage feet, you got roughly the sound of Cracked Strings.

And then there was Marie. Oh, Marie. She was sitting in Ben's English class, with strands of salmon-colored hair and a smile that looked like it glowed in the dark. Ben had a hopeless crush on her. Of course, he had neither the courage nor a convincing plan to approach her. Instead, when he met her in the hallway, he stammered something stupid like "Hey... uh... nice... uh... book" - even though she wasn't even holding a book in her hand. Situations like that were his specialty.

A small festival was to take place in the school playground at the weekend. Well, festival was an exaggeration - a mini-concert by school bands plus a bake sale by the sixth form. But for Ben and his band, it was a chance to finally perform in front of people who didn't just happen to get lost in the basement. Nervous to the max, of course. Paul said: "This will be our breakthrough!" Lisa asked ironically: "We're more likely to break through the audience's eardrums..."

On the day of the festival, the sun shone as if it wanted to show everyone that it didn't always have to be a spoilsport. The schoolyard was full: pupils, teachers, parents wondering whether they would have been better off attending a soccer match. And in the middle of it all: Marie, with her casual denim jacket, eyeing the guitar of another band's performance with interest.

Ben was sweating profusely. He was standing behind the small stage, which actually only consisted of a few wooden platforms. Paul patted him on the shoulder: "Hey, chill. If it gets really shit, we'll just run away." It wasn't an uplifting tip, but at least it was honest. Lisa distortedly tuned her keyboard synth, which sounded like a computer sneezing.

Then the big moment: The Cracked Strings took to the stage. A bit of applause, mainly from their own friends. Ben saw Marie in the crowd. His heart was racing. The first song: a self-written piece entitled "Lost in a Lunchbreak", about the boring school day. The beginning: bumpy. Paul missed the cue, Lisa played two notes too high. Ben swallowed, looked at Marie - and at that moment, when their eyes met briefly, he played a chord cleanly, clearly, almost beautifully.

Somehow they caught themselves. The song rolled along, shakily at first, then with increasing confidence. The other bands looked surprised, as if a damaged Trabi had suddenly mutated into a sports car. The audience listened. Some nodded to the beat. And Marie smiled. Ben thought he was in a dream.

During the second song, which actually consisted of three chords, something like enthusiasm set in. A few pupils clapped, a teacher tapped his chin as if to say: "Not bad at all!" And Marie began to dance lightly, her hair blowing in the gentle wind. Ben's fingers found the strings as if by magic and he played as if he had done nothing else all his life. Maybe it was a bit of imagination, but who cared right now?

At the end of their little show, there was even a good round of applause. No one threw tomatoes at her, no one shouted "Stop it!". A quiet wave of appreciation spread. Ben could feel his cheeks glowing red, but it was a good feeling. Paul threw the sticks in the air, Lisa grinned broadly and Ben smiled shyly. Being happy felt damn good.

When they came off the stage, Marie suddenly stood in front of Ben. "Hey, your guitar sounded really nice. I didn't know you could play so well." Ben swallowed, trying to find his voice and not talk nonsense: "Thanks... er... well... thanks!" Marie laughed. "You really have talent. And you should get on with it!"

Paul and Lisa gave Ben a quick wink and tactically withdrew to give the two of them space. Marie ran her fingers through her hair. "Maybe you can show me how to finger these chords?" asked her, and Ben was sure he was about to burst into a thousand bubbles with happiness.

Just a few weeks ago, Ben felt like an average teenager without a plan. Now there he was, with a guitar, a band that at least started to work, and the girl of his dreams who was interested in him. Sure, this wasn't a Hollywood fairytale, more like the low-budget version of one, but it was real. It was good.

As the sun sank lower, Ben and Marie sat down on the upturned wooden bench behind the stage. He played a few notes, she tried to follow suit, laughing at her own mistakes. It was no longer a silly crush, but something that felt real. And so a few circles came full circle for Ben: He had found a piece of happiness, in himself and in music. He belonged, perhaps not yet as a great guitar hero, but as someone who was simply allowed to be himself.

And so this day did not end in disaster, but in a small personal happy ending: he had done what he could, and it had been enough. He had overcome his insecurity, Marie smiled at him, and the music, bumpy and quirky, had given them a moment strong enough to make them forget all the everyday nonsense.

Ben didn't know what tomorrow would bring, but right now it didn't matter. He had found his place - at least for the moment. And if that wasn't a happy ending, then what was?

A HEART UNDER EVERY LAYER

He was rarely seen without his insecure smile: Jonas, in his early twenties, a young man with soft, round features, which he always covered up with loose clothing. He was the one everyone called "nice". The solid friend, the good guy, the one who never said no when someone needed help - but also the one who never stood out. Invisible behind his "niceness", which many took for granted.

Jonas wasn't just carrying around a few extra kilos; he was carrying the doubts, the insecurities, the feeling of never really being seen. His friends liked him, but they rarely asked how he was really doing. Most girls came to him to talk themselves out, about their problems with other guys, but rarely to get to know him. He was the fat, nice guy, the "buddy" whose value seemed to lie only in his reliable presence.

But fate is sometimes headstrong. One day, Marie came into his life. She wasn't the type of person who had "Fateful Encounter" emblazoned across her head in bright letters right from the start. Rather modest, reserved, with a certain gentleness that impressed Jonas without him immediately realizing it. They had mutual acquaintances and got lost in conversation in a secret corner at a party. Somehow the chemistry was right without being able to put your finger on it.

The special thing was not a dramatic moment, but this strange lightness when they talked to each other. Both were basically quiet people who thought more than they said. It was different with Marie: Jonas found that he could find words to express his inner self. He talked about his childhood, about the teasing about his weight, about his fear of always being second best. And Marie listened. Really listened. Not out of politeness, but out of genuine interest.

They met more often. Not romantic candlelit dinners, but long drives in the car. Marie still lived with her parents and sometimes, if the evening progressed too quickly, Jonas would park outside the house while she went inside to get something to eat and then they would talk together. Often they didn't end up in the house, but stayed in the car, the hood steamed up by the night-time haze, the streetlights casting pale beams of light onto the empty streets.

These nightly conversations became a ritual. Jonas and Marie sat in his old, slightly musty car, which smelled of chewing gum and upholstery cleaning, and talked until the stars faded in the sky. About everything and nothing: her fears, her dreams, his insecurities about his appearance, her doubts as to whether she would ever break out of her family's narrow expectations. They supported each other without having to say it.

Jonas noticed how something changed in her presence: he no longer had to play the nice, harmless teddy bear in order to be liked. He was allowed to be himself - with all his doubts, desires and feelings. And Marie opened up too. She, who was so often unsure whether she was good enough, clever enough, strong enough, found in Jonas someone who accepted her as she was. Her voice trembled less, her laughter sounded freer when she spoke to him.

It wasn't that cheesy Hollywood love that sparks at the first moment. It was something more intimate, deeper, almost like a sibling relationship, but with that fine spark that was more than platonic. They became constant companions, confidants who showed their mental scars without fear of ridicule. Marie was like a sister to Jonas that he never had - and yet more than that, a friend for life, a companion.

Over time, Jonas learned that it wasn't wrong to express his feelings. He didn't always have to hide all his wishes behind a cheerful nod. Marie encouraged him to be honest when something didn't suit him. "You're good the way you are," she once said when he complained about his broad shoulders. "That's not your flaw, it's a part of you - a part I like no less than the rest."

He began to question his surroundings. Why did he always remain the nice guy with no needs of his own? Why did he get involved in relationships with people who didn't really see him? Marie showed him how valuable he was - not as a service station for others, but as a person with his own dignity. She became his blueprint: he wanted to preserve this feeling of mutual respect for future friendships, relationships and encounters.

And Marie also benefited. Through Jonas, she learned that she didn't have to do everything to meet her parents' expectations. She found the courage to go her own way. "If you stand up for yourself, you're never wrong," said Jonas when she was pondering whether she should change her unloved degree course. His gentleness, his sense of subtlety gave her security. She appreciated his softness, his thoughtfulness. He was like a safe shore for her, where she could dock when the current of life became too strong.
Their solidarity was like a warm light in an often cold world. They spent many more nights in this old car, in

front of the family home, with soft music in the background. A friendship developed, an intimate tenderness that didn't need any strenuous explanations. He sometimes visited her during the day, drank tea in her room and showed her old photo albums. They went for walks together, laughed about little things that seemed trivial to others.

Every day they grew beyond their limits. He began to look for clothes that didn't hide his figure, but comfortably hugged it. She dared to tell her parents that she wanted to study something other than what they had planned. They supported each other, gave each other the courage they would not have mustered on their own.

At some point, on a cool spring evening, as the scent of freshly blossoming flowers wafted through the air, they realized that they had shown each other the path that would make them both stronger and more self-confident. Jonas felt that he was no longer a "fat, nice guy", but simply Jonas, a person with heart, pride and perspective. And Marie was no longer the shy girl, but a young woman with her own plans, standing on her own two feet.

They smiled at each other in the semi-dark car where they had shared so much. This time there was no uncertainty in their gazes, but warmth. A warmth that transcended boundaries: friendship, affection, perhaps love - it all merged into a feeling of deep intimacy. The night shone brighter, as if even the stars knew that something precious had been created here.

The happy ending was not a big firework display, not a staged finale. It was this gentle arrival at oneself, in the eyes of the other. Jonas and Marie had matured, had exchanged their fears for understanding and support. He now knew that people who appreciated him were guided by his inner values - his honesty, his empathy. And she knew that she had permission to stand up for herself.

At some point, when the sun was about to rise, they drove slowly down the road. The radio played soft music and they sat there hand in hand, the wind in their faces. They had freed each other from old chains, and that was more than any dramatic confession of love. It was a happy ending that was allowed to last - because they had learned what trust, respect and appreciation meant.

In the future, Jonas would remember Marie when he met new people, would check whether they reciprocated this respect. And Marie would always know that she had the strength to go her own way, supported by the man who had become more than just a friend. Together, they made the world a little warmer that evening, and their souls had finally arrived.

THE LUMINOUS THREADS

On a remote outpost, somewhere on the edge of the explorable universe, a strange creature drifted through the empty hull of an abandoned spaceship. It was not a human, not a robot, not a creature that a cataloged biologist would immediately recognize. It could have been described as some kind of gelatinous lump, but that would not have been true to its true nature. It was more like a bundle of living, glowing threads, pulsating and dancing around each other. We simply call it *The Core*.

The core was lonely. Ever since he had woken up in this ship, he had known nothing but silence, metal corridors and the dull stillness between the stars. He didn't know who he was or why he was here, only that he existed, somewhere between the mechanical groaning of ventilation shafts and sparks of obsolete electronics.

One day, while gliding weightlessly through a narrow corridor, he discovered something new: a strange device, not much bigger than a human head, with a round screen and lots of wires. As *The Core* approached, the device flickered. A distorted voice croaked, as if trying to say something across infinite distances. *The core* felt curiosity, a tickle in its strings. He approached cautiously.

After a few glitches, the device showed a tiny image: a human being. Not alive, but an old recording. A young man was laughing, holding his stomach as if he had experienced something incredibly funny. *The core* did not know this "laughter", but the sound awakened a warm tingling in his fibers. He stayed to watch.

The recording showed other scenes: People smiling, hugging each other, telling stories. *Kern* watched for hours, oblivious to the emptiness around him. He saw how hands touched, how faces took on soft features when they came close to each other. He didn't understand every detail, but he sensed that these beings were important to each other. That there was such a thing as closeness, even in the darkness.

It took days for *The Core* to realize that he didn't have to be alone. Maybe there were others out there somewhere who could give him that strange feeling he felt at the sight of people laughing. But the ship was empty, and he had no legs to go far, no words to call out. Just his shimmering threads and the desire to find someone who appreciated his presence.

One morning, if there was such a thing as morning in the darkness of space, he made contact with the device again. He touched a wire with a delicate fiber. Suddenly a jolt went through the ship. Some old emergency generator kicked in, an auxiliary signal was activated, inaudible to most, but somewhere, deep in the void, a radio relay picked up the pulse.

Days later, a small rescue capsule docked. A lone traveler, a collector of rare relics by trade, followed the strange distress call. He climbed out of his capsule and felt his way through the silent corridors. Then he saw *The Core*. He was startled at first. But *The Core* lit up gently, as if to say: "Please, don't be afraid."
The traveler, a human named Elion, was not stupid. He saw that this being was not threatening him, but was looking at him curiously. So he sat down carefully, hovered in the low artificial gravity field and began to speak half aloud. Surprised, he realized that *The Core*

was reacting to his words, the threads trembling, glowing.

Elion found the old recording device and played the videos. *The core* "listened" again, this time alongside a living listener. Elion told stories of starports where travelers met, traded, laughed. He spoke of communities living peacefully side by side. *The core*, though wordless, shone brighter, as if soaking up every word.

After a while, Elion wondered if *The Core* wanted to come along. The ship was a tomb of metal, there was nothing here to nourish this creature. So he opened a transport box, and *The Core* wriggled carefully inside, as if to say, "Yes, please, take me with you. I don't want to be alone anymore."

They left the dead ship and glided out into the darkness, towards a space station where lights flashed, voices echoed and music played. For *Der Kern*, everything was strange, but exciting. Elion carried him through the corridors like a treasure, showing him how people hugged each other, how they laughed, how they acted, argued and made up again.

People were skeptical at first. The shimmering bundle of glowing threads was unusual. But when they saw how Elion spoke to it, how *The Core* pulsated gently when someone said kind words, they perked up. Children ran after him giggling, adults looked at him curiously. And little by little, a feeling of acceptance grew in this small community.

Over the weeks, *The Core* learned to use its signals more intelligibly. When he felt joy, his threads shimmered in soft pastel shades. When he was astonished, short sparks shot up. The ward became his new home, a place full of colors, sounds, smells - and above all, full of life.

One evening, as Elion and *The Core* gazed out of a window at the stars together, the creature felt something like inner peace for the first time. It was no longer alone. It had found a home, a handful of friends who cherished it, even without language, without a familiar form. It was now part of a community, just like the people in the photographs.

And so the circle was complete: an unknown being, born of loneliness and silence, had finally found warmth and a sense of belonging. The shining threads vibrated gently, as if they were smiling. Yes, thought Elion, no journey ended here - rather, a new life began here, one in which understanding and joy could spread across all borders.

This was perhaps not the story that anyone had expected. But therein lay its magic: a being without a voice, a strange bundle of light, had found a happy ending. And in the glow of its threads, the future shone brighter than all the stars in the infinite universe.

A PIECE OF HEAVEN

The sun fell in narrow strips through the curtains of the children's room, where everything looked as if someone had frozen time. The stuffed animal with the bent ear, the half-colored pictures in the sketchbook, the crumbs on the floor from a candy bar she had eaten the day before yesterday - everything looked as if it could come back to life at any moment, as if Mom could walk in the door and ask if everything was okay.

But mom wouldn't come in anymore. The silence in the house was louder than any crying. The world had seemed gray for days, even though it was spring. Dad often just sat on the sofa, his eyes on the floor. Aunts and uncles came by, bringing food, saying quiet words that no one really heard. And the child - let's call her Lea - didn't understand every whispered word from the adults, but knew that mom wouldn't be coming back.

Lea stood at the window, her forehead pressed against the cool glass, and looked out onto the garden where she used to play with Mama. Mom had shown her how to weave daisies into little crowns. Now there were only empty garden chairs and a bird singing on the fence. Lea listened to it, and there was something in its song that she couldn't put her finger on - perhaps a tiny spark of comfort.

She didn't want Mama to be forgotten. And yet she felt something ache inside her when she thought of Mama's smile, of her warm hands, of her gentle voice. It was as if there was now a hole in her heart, a hole through which the wind whistled and made her shiver. She didn't know how to fix something like that.

Her father came into the room and sat down on the carpet with her. He had red-rimmed eyes, but he smiled, as carefully as if he had forgotten how. He put his arm around her and said nothing for a while. Then he whispered: "Mom is still with us, just in a different place. No longer here in the house, but in our memories, in everything she taught us."

Lea didn't quite understand how mom could be there when she was away. But she felt the warmth in her father's arms and knew that she wasn't alone. Perhaps they could think of Mama together, tell her stories, sing the songs she had hummed so often. Perhaps a piece of Mama lived on in every laugh, in every loving gesture.

Over the next few days, Lea searched for clues. She found Mama's scarf in the wardrobe, smelled it as if she could catch the familiar scent. She leafed through an old photo album, saw Mama as a young girl, later Mama with her as a baby in her arms. She drew a picture of Mama surrounded by flowers and hung it above her bed.

At night, she sometimes dreamed that Mama came to her bedside and gently stroked her forehead, as she used to do when Lea had a fever. In her dream, Mom would say in a soft voice: "You can do it. You are not alone. My heart beats in yours." And when Lea woke up, she no longer felt quite so empty, as if the memory had filled her up again.

Over time, the pain didn't go away completely, but it changed. A sharp blade became something blunter, something you could touch with your hand without completely fading away. Lea discovered that she was able to talk about Mama without immediately bursting into tears. She told her father about Mama's favorite song, she hummed it softly in the garden and the bird on the fence seemed to be listening.

One afternoon, as the sun fell through the curtains again and a dusty golden light floated in the room, Lea smiled at a photo of mom handing her an ice cream. She felt a gentle warmth in her stomach, as if she had understood that love doesn't disappear just because someone is no longer there. Love remained, even if it hurt. And this love gave her the strength to go on.

Her father sat down with her and held her hand. "We will always tell mom's story," he said. "In our laughter, in what we do, in the things she taught us. She will always be a part of us, Lea." The girl nodded, wiping a tear from her cheek. The tear tasted salty, but the pain in it was no longer as helpless as it had been at first.

In the days that followed, Lea began to play a little again, with her doll, or she practiced weaving daisy chains herself. These were faltering steps back into life, but she felt that she could do it. She could be sad and still hope. She could miss mom and still grow.

Sometimes she looked up at the sky in the evening, looking for a star that shone brighter than the others. She imagined that Mama could be up there. The thought was childlike and yet comforting. And when she found the star, she smiled softly. It was as if she had a piece of the sky all to herself - and with it a piece of Mama that she would never leave.

The weeks went by and Lea learned to deal with her loss. She no longer cried every day, but when she did, it was okay. She could talk to her father about it, about Mama's favorite foods, about her laughter, about the words she made up when she was happy. Every sentence kept the memory alive and made Lea stronger.

One sunny afternoon, as she sat in the garden making a wreath of daisies, the wind seemed to gently brush through her hair. She smiled, thinking of mom. The pain was there, but also gratitude, love and hope. She now knew that even when someone leaves, something precious stays behind. Mom's love lived on in her, a warm light that would accompany her on her way.

IN THE SHADOW OF THE NORTH WIND

In a remote small town, where the winters were long and the wind drowned out almost everything else, lived a man who shaped his everyday life quietly yet powerfully. His life was not played out on grand stages, but in rooms filled with voices, stories and quiet moments. He was part of the heartbeat of the community, althhough he never said it out loud.

Every morning, before the city really woke up, he made his way to a place that focused his life like a burning glass. Ideas, perspectives and generations collided here. Between the creaking floors and the smell of chalk , connections were formed that were as invisible as they were significant. His place was not in the front row, but in the quiet corners, where he had a clear view of everything.

He was a bridge builder, someone who knew how to connect the heaviness of the past with the restlessness of the present. Stories and language were his tools, but he used them not with the sharpness of a chisel, but with the precision of a quill. He told of old times, of things lost, but always with an eye to the future.

His life was not only characterized by words and memories. There was this quiet fascination with technology that captivated him time and again. While others relied on the familiar, he immersed himself in digital worlds, exploring possibilities that were not visible to everyone. For him, technology was not an end in itself, but a tool to create something new - be it a small impulse in everyday life or something bigger that quietly resonated.

But the special thing was that he never forgot where he came from. The places he loved were not the noisy metropolises, but the quiet, almost unreal landscapes of the north. The wind that blew there sometimes seemed like a part of his thoughts - powerful, irrepressible, but also cleansing. It was not difficult to imagine him standing in a place where only the sound of the sea and the cries of seagulls broke the silence as he contemplated what lay ahead.

For him, music was more than just sound. It was a space in which he could express himself when words were not enough. On quiet nights, when the world came to rest, melodies arose in him that spoke of vastness and thoughtfulness. He knew that they never had to be played out loud to be heard.

His dealings with people were characterized by respect and a deep calm. He often saw more than he showed, often understood more than he said. He was not someone who had to solve problems out loud - his solutions often lay in a sentence, a look, a moment of listening. It was this quiet presence that made people seek him out, be it for advice, comfort or simply to be heard.

He was no less extraordinary in his private life. He lived in a way that was unusual for many, but natural for him: separate from the person closest to him, yet in an intimate connection that others rarely achieved. It was an arrangement that left room for independence and yet was full of deep closeness. In these moments of togetherness - be it conversations or shared silences - he found a balance that strengthened him.

There was also another side that not everyone saw. A side that sometimes doubted, that searched, that wondered whether the path he was taking was the right one. But he didn't let these doubts win. Instead, he used them to develop himself further, to keep finding new opportunities, for himself and for others.

It was not his style to take center stage. He was not a leader who gave orders with a loud voice, but someone who stayed the course, even when the wind was blowing hard. People who knew him might describe him as quiet or thoughtful, but the truth was that he had a strength about him that didn't need to be loud to make an impact.

The days in the city passed, the seasons changed, and his life flowed on like a quiet, steady stream. And yet he left his mark, sometimes unnoticed, sometimes obvious. Be it in the minds of those who heard his stories, in the hearts of those who felt his music, or in the ideas he passed on in quiet words.

In the shadow of the north wind lived a man whose work was invisible to many, but whose presence remained irreplaceable. He was a silent compass, a shining line in an often gray world. And while the wind continued to blow, he carried with him all the stories, melodies and thoughts that defined him, in a way that few could truly understand.

FOUND IN THE FLAMES

The sky was a dirty gray that never cleared, streaked with black smoke rising from the burnt remains of a once-living city. Not a bird flew, not a tree rustled, only the sound of footsteps on broken glass and the occasional thunder of cannons could be heard. Here, in the rutted ruins, the soldier had long since lost hope.

He was no more than a shadow of what he had once been. His name - once worn with pride - was now nothing more than a whisper in his own head. He was one of many, swallowed by the maw of a war that had no meaning and knew no victors. His uniform was tattered, his helmet cracked, and his rifle felt heavier than the world itself.

The soldier was alone. His unit had been torn apart in a final, senseless battle. Friends, comrades - they were all gone, left behind in the cold of the trenches or under the rubble that the war had left behind like the tracks of a beast. The world was empty, and with it his heart seemed to be nothing but a hollow space.

For days he wandered through the ruins, searching for nothing in particular. Food was scarce, water a precious commodity, but the worst thing was the silence inside him. Hopelessness ate through his thoughts like a poison. He wondered why he kept going at all. Why not just stop, let himself sink into the dust and welcome the inevitable?

Then he heard it. A sound, faint, almost swallowed up by the screeching of the wind. He paused, listened. A whimper, a soft cry. It sounded like a child, lost among the rubble. His heart tightened - he had never expected to hear a human voice again that wasn't full of hate. With a spark of hope that he barely understood, he followed the sound.

He found her between collapsed walls. A little girl, barely older than eight, with a dirty face and trembling shoulders. She had huddled in the corner of a ruined house, her hands clutched tightly around a torn doll. Her eyes - large and full of fear - were fixed on him as if he were another monster that had come out of the flames.

He knelt down, slowly, put the rifle aside. His voice was rough from days without words. "Don't be afraid," he said softly. "I won't hurt you." The girl stared at him, and for a moment the only response was the quivering of her lips. But then she pushed the doll a little tighter against her and nodded barely perceptibly.

He took her with him. It wasn't a conscious decision, more an instinct that guided him. She was alone, like him, and in her fear he recognized his own. They barely spoke, walking through the ruins in silence, looking for shelter, for food. Sometimes she would point to something - an intact can, a crooked window that offered shelter - and he marveled at how observant she was.

Gradually, the silence between them gave way to a quiet exchange. She told him about her family, about a brother who had disappeared, about her mother, whom she had lost on the run. He listened without saying much, but her words gave him back something he thought he had lost long ago: a reason to go on.

One night, when they were hiding in the rubble of an old school, he dared to ask: "How did you manage to survive alone for so long?" She looked at him with wide, serious eyes. "I believed in the doll. Mom said it would protect me." She held the tattered toy out to him and he smiled weakly. For her, this doll was a talisman, a piece of normality in a world that had long since fallen apart at the seams.

Days turned into weeks, and they kept finding little miracles: a spring of clear water, a store of supplies left behind by others. With every step, his mind became lighter, his thoughts clearer. The girl was his anchor, his task. She needed him, and in that need he found something greater than the war around them: hope.

But the war spared no one. One morning, as they were crossing a ruined village, they heard the sound of engines. A troop of soldiers approached, men with determined looks and heavy weapons. He pushed the girl into the cover of a wall and reached for his rifle. His heart pounded, the fear returned. But he knew he had to protect her at all costs.

But then something unexpected happened. The soldiers stopped, dismounted and the leader - a man with tired eyes - shouted: "You have to get out of here! The front is approaching." His voice was rough, but not hostile. The soldier hesitated, looked at the girl, then stepped forward. "We're looking for shelter," he said, his voice trembling slightly. "I have a child with me."

The leader looked at him for a long time, as if searching for something in him. Finally he nodded. "Come with us. We don't have much, but enough for you." The soldiers were not enemies, but survivors like them, tired of the violence and willing to show humanity, at least for a moment. It was a strange alliance, born of shared need, but it worked.
Over the next few days, they marched together, a small group of people who supported each other. The

girl found new allies, new faces that made her laugh. And the soldier? He felt the weight on his shoulders lighten. The war was not over yet, but in the turmoil he had found something he had never expected: Hope and solidarity.

That evening, as they sat together by the fire, he watched the girl playing with one of the soldiers. He smiled, a genuine smile that had become foreign to him. The war had taken a lot, but at that moment he felt that all was not lost. Sometimes, he thought, a single spark is enough to break through the darkness. And it was this spark that had saved him and the girl.

THE FOREND OF THE UNIVERSE

Eibelshausen was a sleepy nest in Hesse, where time flowed at a leisurely pace and the stories were bigger than the streets. Most of the inhabitants were content with their lives: they drank their cider, tended their gardens and swapped anecdotes that everyone had heard a hundred times before. But not young Tillmann. For him, Eibelshausen was a trap, a prison of routine and boredom.

Tillmann was a good-for-nothing, at least in the eyes of the old women who peeked out from behind the curtains as he strolled along the cobbled streets. "What's going to happen to that boy?" they whispered behind closed doors. He wore holey pants, always had a strange story on his lips and was mildly ridiculed by the adults at because of his restlessness. Tillmann wanted more. And he knew that "more" was waiting for him somewhere out there.

His search began on a windy evening in late fall, when the branches of the trees reached for the sky like fingers. He was sitting in the dilapidated barn on the outskirts of the village, the meeting place of his sparse clique. But that evening he was alone. In his hand he held a crumpled old book that he had discovered in the depths of the village library. It was called "The Hidden Legends of Hesse" and was a collection of myths, stories and obscure tales.

One passage in particular fascinated him: According to legend, there was a relic of cosmic significance in the district of Eibelshausen - the universe plug. An inconspicuous but magical bathtub plug which, if pulled, would cause the universe to collapse in on itself. The exact location was given in the legend as the "Steimel", a hill overgrown with brambles and old undergrowth.

The story sounded crazy, but in Tillmann's head it began to blaze like a spark in dry grass. An adventure - a real adventure - could be exactly what snapped his life out of its rut. He read the passage again, then a third time, and each word sounded like a challenge: "Find the forend. Find the impossible."

The next morning he set off, equipped with an old map that he had torn out of the book and a rucksack full of random things: a pocket knife, a bottle of water, a compass that never worked properly and a flashlight that was almost empty. "You're a fool," he muttered to himself, "but a fool with a mission."

The Steimel lay on the edge of a forest that was avoided by the villagers. It was said to be home to foxes with glowing eyes and strange creatures that appeared when the moon was full. Tillmann knew that most of the stories only served to keep children in the villages, but something about the silence of the forest made him shiver.

He followed the instructions on the map, which was barely legible, and cut his way through thorny undergrowth. Hours passed and the sun slowly crept across the sky until he finally reached a clearing. There, in the midst of trees and stone boulders, rose the Steimel. It was not an impressive mound, more of a gentle hill, but something about it seemed... strange.

When Tillmann reached the foot of the hill, he heard a whisper. At first he thought it was the wind blowing through the trees, but it sounded like words, unintelligible sounds that penetrated deep into his head. "It's just tiredness," he mumbled, but he couldn't help feeling that someone was watching him.

The bottom of the steimel was covered in moss, and in the center was a circular depression that looked like an old fireplace. Stones lay there in strange patterns, and as Tillmann stepped closer, he noticed that they bore symbols. They were carved, their edges worn by time, but they glowed faintly in a pulsating blue.

Tillmann knelt down, stroked the stones with his fingers and felt a slight warmth emanating from them. It was as if they were alive. His heart beat faster. Was this the place the legend spoke of? Was the Stulp really here? He began to turn the stones over, hoping to find something, but after minutes of searching there was nothing but cold moss and earth beneath them.

Just as he was about to lean back in discouragement, a twig cracked behind him. Tillmann wheeled around, pocket knife in hand, although he didn't know how it would help him. But it wasn't a wild animal standing in front of him, but a man. He wore a worn coat and his face was scarred. His eyes glittered like steel and he held a long walking stick in his hand.

"You're looking for the forend," the man said in a voice as rough as the crunching of gravel under heavy boots. Tillmann swallowed, unable to say anything. The stranger nodded as if he already knew the answer. "You're not the first person to look for him. But do you know what you're risking?"

"Who are you?" Tillmann finally asked, his voice trembling slightly.

The man smiled wryly. "A wanderer. A collector of stories. And a friend, if you're smart enough to accept the offer."

Tillmann didn't know if he could trust him, but something about the man felt familiar, almost as if he was part of the legend himself. "What do you know about the Stulp?"

"More than you," said the man. "And enough to warn you: if you find it, don't pull it. The universe is not as stable as it seems."

Tillmann's heart hammered in his chest. He knew that this was the beginning of something big - bigger than he could ever have imagined. And as dusk fell over the Steimel, he knew that he would need this man, this enigmatic wanderer, by his side.

The search for the Universe Stulp had begun, and nothing would ever be the same again.

The night on the Steimel was quiet, but not calm. Tillmann and the stranger - who only introduced himself as Johann - sat at the edge of the clearing, the faint glow of the stones in the background. Tillmann had a thousand questions, but Johann remained taciturn. He whittled at a branch with a knife and only spoke when it was absolutely necessary.

"Why are you looking for the forend?" Johann finally asked, without lifting his eyes from his carving.

"Because I can," Tillmann replied defiantly. But when Johann looked at him with those steely gray eyes, he sighed and added more quietly: "Because I want to do something that counts. Something bigger than the boring life in Eibelshausen."

Johann nodded as if he had expected this answer. "The forend is bigger than you can imagine. But size comes with responsibility. When you find the forend, you'll be faced with a choice." He let the words hang in the air without explaining what he meant.

They continued their search the next morning. Johann led Tillmann deeper into the forest, along winding paths that were not on the map. "The Stulp is not an object you can just find," Johann explained. "It's protected - by the Earth, by the universe itself. Only those who are ready can see it."

Tillmann had no idea what that meant, but he kept his mouth shut and followed. The forest seemed to change with every step. The air became heavier, the ground uneven. Shadows seemed to move, although no branches stirred. The back of Tillmann's neck tingled and he had the feeling that he was being watched.

Finally, they reached a deep hollow surrounded by high rocks. In the middle was a small stone altar, overgrown with moss and ivy. Johann held Tillmann back. "This is where my path ends," he said. "If you really want the Stulp, you'll have to go on alone."
"Why?" asked Tillmann, but Johann just shook his head. "Some paths have to be walked alone."
Tillmann felt a knot in his stomach, but he stepped forward. The air around the altar seemed to vibrate and the whispering returned - louder, clearer than before. It was as if dozens of voices were speaking in a jumble, words he couldn't understand, and yet one of them seemed to be calling him.

He reached the altar and saw that there was a round, smooth object in the center. It was no bigger than an apple and shone in a dull, silvery light. It was the universe forend. His heart raced and he reached out. But before he could touch it, a flash of light flashed through the air and a figure appeared in front of him.

It was not a human being, but something else, something ethereal. The figure seemed to consist of light and shadow at the same time, its form constantly changing. A voice spoke, clear and deep: "You have found the gauntlet, but are you ready to carry it?"

Tillmann stepped back, the words echoing in his head. "Ready? Ready for what?" he asked, his voice trembling with a mixture of fear and curiosity.

The figure tilted his head as if pondering his question. "The gauntlet is more than a relic. It is a key, a judgment, an end and a beginning. Its power can preserve or destroy the universe. The one who finds it must decide whether he can bear this responsibility."

Tillmann felt his mouth feel dry. This was not what he had imagined. A magical stopper, yes, but not a galactic responsibility that placed the fate of everything that existed in his hands. "I just wanted to find him," he muttered. "I didn't know..., that."

The figure stepped closer, and although it had no solid body, Tillmann felt an unexpected warmth. "Hope, despair, greed - many have sought the Stulp, but few have reached it. You are here because you are searching within yourself. You wanted to find something that would give your life meaning."

Tillmann nodded slowly. That was true, he knew that. But was he really ready to hold something so big in his hands? He looked over his shoulder to where Johann was still standing at the edge of the clearing, his hands in his pockets as if he knew exactly what Tillmann was going through.

"And if I take it? If I pull the forend?" Tillmann finally asked.

The figure hesitated for a moment. "Then the universe becomes what you carry within you. If it is destruction, it will fall. If it is hope, it will rise again. What are you, Tillmann?"

The question hit him like a blow. What was he? A scallywag from a small village, a dreamer, an adventurer without a plan? He didn't know. His hands trembled as he looked at the forend, which was now glowing almost unrealistically in the middle of the altar.

"I am..." he began, but the words wouldn't come.

Suddenly, a sound penetrated the silence - a humming, deep and menacing. Tillmann and the figure turned around, and three men stepped out of the shadows of the forest. They wore black coats and their faces were covered by scarves. One of them was holding a strange weapon that looked like a cross between a rifle and a blade.

"Step back!" one of them shouted in a voice that cut through Tillmann's marrow. "The forend is not yours!"

Johann was at Tillmann's side in a flash, walking stick in hand. "The guards," he muttered. "I was hoping they wouldn't show themselves."

"Who are they?" asked Tillmann as the men slowly approached.

"Those who believe that the universe belongs only to them," Johann replied. "But we don't have time for explanations. You have to decide, Tillmann. Take the forend - or leave it."

Tillmann looked back and forth between Johann, the figure and the guards. His heart was pounding. The whispers of the forest seemed to grow louder, the world around him swayed as if it were an image that was slowly dissolving.

"I don't know if I can do it," Tillmann said quietly as the guards came closer and closer. Their footsteps crunched on the stones and their presence seemed to make the air heavier. The figure of light and shadow tilted its head as if it sensed his doubts.

"No one is ready when they are faced with their destiny," she said. "But courage is not the absence of fear, but the decision to act in spite of fear."

Johann put a hand on Tillmann's shoulder. "You wanted to find something that counts. Now you have the chance. But be aware: if you decide, you can't go back. The forend becomes your responsibility and you will have to live with the consequences - whatever they are."

Tillmann looked at the forend. It still shone in its strange, silvery light, an inconspicuous thing that nevertheless held the fate of the universe within it. The guards approached, their weapons ready. Tillmann knew there was no turning back.

"I'll do it," he finally said and held out his hand.

The moment his fingers touched the forend, the world seemed to explode. A flash of light broke through the darkness, so bright that it made Tillmann close his eyes. The earth shook and a booming sound filled the air, as if the universe itself was crying out.

When Tillmann opened his eyes again, the world around him had changed. The guards had disappeared, the clearing was empty except for Johann and the figure. But the gauntlet was now in his hand, a weight that felt heavier than it looked.

"It's done," said the figure. "But this is just the beginning. The Stulp has chosen you, Tillmann. You now bear his burden and his power."

Tillmann felt a wave of energy flowing through his body. He saw things he couldn't understand - stars going out, planets being born, the universe itself moving in endless patterns. He felt a connection to everything that existed and it was overwhelming.

"What now?" he finally asked, his voice weak.

Johann smiled wryly. "Now you're going home, boy. You'll need time to understand what you're holding. But don't forget: you're not alone."

The figure nodded. "The universe is full of stories, Tillmann. Your story has only just begun. But be warned: there will be those who seek you out, who want the Stulp for themselves. Be vigilant and act with wisdom."

With these words, the figure began to fade until it finally disappeared. Johann placed a hand on Tillmann's shoulder. "I will stand by your side for as long as I can. But this is your path."

Tillmann nodded. He felt small and yet stronger than ever before. The gauntlet in his hand pulsed slightly, as if it were alive, and Tillmann knew that his search was over - and yet had only just begun.

As he descended the Steimel with Johann, he thought of Eibelshausen, of the quiet streets and the people who would never suspect the burden he was now carrying. But he knew that he would return - not as the good-for-nothing they knew, but as someone who had found something greater.

And in the shadows of the forest, in the infinite expanse of the universe, the next chapters of his story were waiting, ready to be written by him.

THE FORGOTTEN GARDEN

The gravel crunched under her shoes as she walked along the narrow path. It was a cold, gray morning, and the wind carried with it the scent of damp earth and withered leaves. Anna paused briefly to look at the gate in front of her - rusty, half collapsed, a relic from another time. This was it, the entrance to the garden she had once called her paradise.

She hadn't been here for over fifty years. After the death of her parents, the old house had been sold and the garden, once full of life, had been forgotten. But today, at seventy, Anna felt she had to return. Something drew her here, a fleeting feeling, a quiet call from the past.

She pushed the gate open and the sound of the rusty hinges broke the silence. The garden lay before her, overgrown with undergrowth and thorny bushes, the former paths barely recognizable. The large chestnut trees were still standing, their branches like arms reaching out for her. Anna pulled her scarf tighter around her neck and stepped inside.

Every step brought back memories. This was the place where her mother had once planted herbs. She could almost smell the scent of rosemary and thyme, even though all that was left were withered bushes. Further back, under the old willow, her father had read to her in the summer evenings. His laughter, deep and warm, echoed in her head.

She walked deeper into the garden, feeling time turning back with every step. There had once been a small pond where the tall grass now grew. Anna remembered the frogs she had caught and released, the dragonflies that hovered over the water like tiny jewels. But now the pond was dry, a pit full of leaves and shade.

"How did it all go so wild?" she muttered, more to herself than to the bare trees around her. But she knew the answer. Time had no mercy, neither on people nor on places.

When Anna reached the back of the garden, she stopped. This is where she had hidden her secrets as a child, little treasures in old cookie tins that she buried underground. She smiled as she thought of how she had seen herself as the guardian of this garden, a little girl with big dreams.

She knelt down and began to push the grass aside with her hands. The ground was hard and cold, but she persevered. After a few minutes, she came across something hard. She carefully dug further until she uncovered a rusty can. Her heart beat faster as she opened the lid.

Inside was a faded photo - her as a child, next to her mother, both laughing. Next to it was a small necklace with a pendant, a gift from her father. Anna held the necklace in her hand, felt the cool metal on her skin, and suddenly she was that child again, running carefree through the garden.

Tears welled up in her eyes, but she smiled. It was as if the memories she had buried here had come to life, a piece of time that she had brought back.

She sat down on a fallen tree trunk, the chain firmly in her hand. The garden was still overgrown, but in her mind it was alive again. She could see the flowers, the colors, the vibrancy it once had. It was a bittersweet

moment - the joy of remembering and the pain of knowing those times would never return.

As the sun set behind the trees, the air became cooler. Anna knew she had to leave, but she felt no pain in
saying goodbye. The garden would always be a part of
her, not as it was now, but as it lived in her memories.
She rose, walked back to the gate and looked back
one last time. "Thank you," she whispered softly, not
sure to whom the words were addressed - perhaps to
the garden, perhaps to the people who had once shared
it with her.

She pulled the gate shut behind her, accompanied by
the sound of the rusty hinges. She held the small chain
in her hand, a tangible piece of the past that she took
with her. And as she walked down the path, she felt not
only the transience of time, but also the permanence of
memories that blossomed within her like a silent garden.

THE WATCHMAKER

The small workshop in the narrow side street was old, its wooden floorboards creaked with every step and the air smelled of oil and metal. Anna, the clockmaker, sat at her workbench, a magnifying glass over her eye, while her skillful hands worked on an old alarm clock. She loved the precision, the patience it took to bring a clockwork back to life. But she also knew that she was only repairing what time was inexorably destroying.

On this rainy afternoon, there was a knock on the door. Anna looked up, surprised - customers rarely came. Most of them preferred new, modern watches to the old timepieces she repaired. She opened the door and looked into the face of a middle-aged man. He wore a worn coat and held a small wooden box in his hands.

"Are you the watchmaker?" he asked in a voice that sounded rough and cautious at the same time. Anna nodded. "Then you're exactly the right person for this watch," he said and handed her the box.

She opened the lid and discovered a pocket watch. The case was made of matt silver and engraved with filigree patterns that looked like interwoven stars. The glass was slightly cracked and the hands stood still. It was a beautiful watch, and yet there was something sinister about it.

"It no longer works," the man explained. "But it is... special. Very special. Can you fix it?" Anna nodded hesitantly. Something about the clock wouldn't let her go, a kind of silent promise that she didn't quite understand.

After the man had left, she sat down at her table and carefully opened the back of the clock. The movement was unlike any she had ever seen. The gears seemed to glow, as if they were made of a different material, and the ticking she heard as the case moved was not steady. It sounded... alive.

Hours passed as she worked to understand the mechanics. Every time she moved a wheel, it seemed as if the air around her changed. The rain outside her window seemed to fall slower, then faster. An uneasy feeling crept up inside her, but she kept working until she had finally repaired the last crack in the glass.

When she put the clock back together, it began to tick. The sound was deeper, almost like a heartbeat. Suddenly Anna felt as if the space around her was blurring. The workshop seemed to flicker, and when she looked up, it was as if she was sitting in the past and the present at the same time.

Anna felt a strange energy emanating from the clock. She picked it up and noticed that the hands were moving backwards. "That can't be," she muttered and placed the clock on the workbench. But as she did so, the world around her flickered again. Suddenly she was no longer in her workshop, but in a bright, sunny meadow that she remembered from her childhood.

She looked around and there she was: a younger self, no more than ten years old, laughing and flying a kite. The wind carried the sound of her own laughter to her, and for a moment Anna forgot everything else. But when she felt the watch in her hand, it pulled her back to reality.

With trembling hands, she placed the clock on the workbench again. She knew now that it was more than just a clock. She could manipulate time, make it flow backwards, bring memories to life. But what did that mean? And what would happen if she continued to use the clock?

The days passed and Anna could not resist the temptation. She set the clock again and found herself in other moments of her past - her first kiss, saying goodbye to her father, the early morning hour when she opened her workshop. It was exhilarating, but also painful.

But the more she used the watch, the more she felt that something was wrong. The transitions became harder, as if time was resisting her. She noticed that it was taking her longer and longer to return to the present, and sometimes the memories she visited seemed to change.

One evening, as she was winding the watch one last time, there was another knock on her door. It was the man who had brought her the watch. But this time his look was more serious. "Did you use the watch?" he asked, and Anna could only nod guiltily at him.

"Then you know she's not a toy," he said. "Time is inevitable, Anna. We can't control it, only flow with it. This watch... it's a test. And now you have to decide."

Anna felt the weight of his words. She looked at the clock lying quietly on the workbench. She knew that she had the chance to relive everything, to get back everything she had lost. But she also knew that by doing so, she could further destroy the course of time.

After a long moment, she reached for the watch - not to wind it up, but to put it back in the wooden box. "I understand," she said quietly. "Time is not mine."

The man nodded, and there was a hint of recognition in his eyes. "You've made the right choice."

When he left the workshop, Anna felt a strange calm. The clock was gone, but she knew that the memories she had visited were with her forever. She didn't have to change the past to live with the present. And as the workshop fell back into the quiet ticking of normal clocks, Anna felt that she had regained control of the most important thing - herself.

THE EMPTY CAFÉ

Every morning, at nine o'clock sharp, he opened the heavy wooden door of the small café on the corner of the deserted main street. The bell above the door rang softly, an inconspicuous sound that would have been lost in a city full of noise and movement. But here, in this café, it was the only sound, apart from the scraping of the chairs on the wooden floorboards and the hissing of the coffee machine behind the counter.

The man, whose name no one seemed to know, took off his coat and hung it on the same hook next to the door. He was middle-aged, with a face that was neither particularly striking nor completely unremarkable. His eyes, however, had a depth that told stories if you looked closely - stories of loss, of endless searching and a constant emptiness that he could not fill.

The café was old-fashioned, almost out of time. Dark wood paneling ran along the walls and the tables were covered with white and red checkered blankets. Heavy curtains hung from the windows, dimming the light so that the room was always bathed in a soft twilight. It was quiet, so quiet that you could hear the ticking of the large wall clock that hung behind the bar.

The man sat down at his regular place - a small table in the far corner, near the window. People rarely walked past outside, and when they did, it seemed as if they didn't even notice the café. It was as if it was in a kind of limbo, hidden from the hustle and bustle of the city.

A cup of coffee appeared in front of him, as always. No one asked him for his order, no one brought the cup, and yet there it was, steaming and perfect. He took a sip, closed his eyes and let the bitter taste melt on his tongue. It was the only moment of the day when he didn't feel completely lost.

He had often tried to speak to the café owner, but he never got an answer. There was always a shadow behind the counter, shadowy and indistinct. The man could never tell whether it was really someone or just an illusion. The silence of the café seemed to swallow everything, even the thoughts he was trying to form.

Every day he stayed for an hour, sometimes longer. He stared out of the window, drank his coffee and let the world pass him by. It was a ritual that he couldn't explain. All he knew was that he had to come back. The café was the only place where he had the feeling that the emptiness inside him wasn't getting any bigger.

But one day something was different. When he opened the door, the room was no longer empty. A woman was sitting at a table near the bar. She had long, dark hair that half covered her face and a book in her hand. The man stopped in the doorway, surprised. He hadn't seen anyone here for years, and yet the woman looked as if she had always been part of the café.

He sat down at his table as usual, but his thoughts were with the stranger. She leafed through her book without looking up, as if she were alone. Finally, he took heart and cleared his throat quietly. "Excuse me," he said.

The woman raised her eyes. Her eyes were deep and dark, and for a moment it seemed as if she could look straight into him. "Yes?" she asked, her voice quiet, almost like a whisper.
"I've never seen anyone here before," the man began hesitantly. "Are you... new?"

The woman smiled slightly. "No, I've been coming here for a long time. Maybe you just haven't looked closely."

The answer confused him. He wanted to ask more, but the words stuck in his throat. Instead, he just nodded and turned back to his coffee. But her presence didn't let him go.

In the days that followed, she kept coming back and he slowly began to talk to her. They talked about books, about the city, about the café. But the more he talked to her, the stranger she became to him. She seemed to know everything about the café - its history, its quirks. But every time he asked her about herself, she evaded him.

"Why are you coming here?" he asked one day.

The woman smiled sadly. "For the same reason as you," she said, "I'm looking for something I've lost."

This answer made him think. What was he looking for? He had no name for it, no clear idea. All he knew was that there was an emptiness that he was trying to fill.

One evening, as he was about to leave the café, she stopped him. "Stay a moment," she said, "I want to show you something."

She led him to the counter, behind which the shadowy figure was still standing motionless. She put her hand on the old wall clock, which was ticking loudly. "This clock," she said, "doesn't just show the time. It shows how much time we have to find something that connects us."

The man stared at the clock. The hands were moving slowly, but they seemed to be flickering, almost hesitating. "What does that mean?" he asked.

The woman smiled. "The café is a place between worlds. It gathers those who are lost and gives them the opportunity to remember what they are looking for."

Suddenly the man understood. The café was no ordinary place, and the woman was no ordinary visitor. She was a part of the café, just as he had become. But while she was aware of it, he hadn't seen it all this time.

He returned the next morning, but the café had disappeared. The corner where it had stood was empty, as if it had never existed. The man stood still for a while, then smiled. The emptiness inside him had not disappeared, but it had become smaller. And something new had grown in its place - a spark of connection, a hint of hope.

THE LAST LETTER

It was a rainy fall afternoon when she found the letter. The bookshop where she worked was almost empty, only the soft rustling of pages and the occasional splash of rain against the windows filled the silence. Anna, in her early thirties, had retreated to the far corner of the store to catalog a box of old books that had just come in.

She discovered the letter among the yellowed pages of a novel. It was carefully folded and obviously old, the ink slightly faded, the envelope without an address. Curiosity drove her to open it, even though she knew it was an invasion of someone's privacy. But the words she found were like an echo from another time, a voice speaking to her through the paper after years.

"Dearest Clara," the letter began. The handwriting was elegant and flowing, and the words sounded like a gentle whisper. It was a declaration of love, full of longing and regret. The writer, a man called Paul, spoke of a mistake he had made, of a farewell that should never have happened, and of a hope that it was not too late to make amends.

Anna read the letter twice, then a third time. There was something about it that stayed with her - the words had a depth that touched her, as if they had been written for her. She wondered why the letter had never been sent. Had Paul changed his mind? Or had Clara never been found?

She couldn't let go of the thought. That same evening, she sat in her small apartment, the letter in front of her on the kitchen table, and thought about what she should do. It would have been easy to put it back in the book and forget about it. But Anna felt that she couldn't do that. The words seemed to be calling her, as if she had a task to fulfill.

Her search began the next day. The letter contained no surnames, no addresses, just clues - a date, a city, some places Paul mentioned. It was like a puzzle, and Anna felt a strange energy as she began to put the pieces together.

Her first lead took her to the town library, where she searched through old town archives. It was laborious, but she found an entry about a Paul who had lived in the town at the same time. He had been a teacher , it said, and he had left the town shortly after the date of the letter.

But Clara remained a mystery. No one seemed to know anything about her. Anna continued to search, talking to older residents who remembered Paul, but Clara seemed to be like a ghost, a trace that disappeared into nothingness.

Weeks passed and Anna felt her hope fading. Perhaps this was a dead end, a story that would never find a resolution. But just as she was about to give up, she found another clue - an old newspaper article about a woman called Clara who had worked as an artist in the 1960s. She had run a small gallery in the city before she suddenly disappeared.

Anna followed this lead and traveled to the neighboring town where Clara had last been seen. She found the old gallery, now a café, and spoke to the owners. An older man remembered Clara. "She was an extraordinary woman," he said. "But she gave up everything one day and left. No one knows where."

It seemed as if Clara and Paul had both been swallowed up by time. But Anna couldn't stop. The letter had changed her, had awakened a longing in her that she couldn't explain. It was as if she had to find out something about herself by searching for Paul and Clara.

Eventually, her journey took her to a small nursing home where she heard that an old man named Paul, who had once been a teacher, lived. Her heart beat faster as she entered the building. The letter was in her pocket, the paper now soft and worn from her hands.

Paul was frail, his eyes tired, but when Anna mentioned the letter, something lit up inside him. She read the words to him and tears ran down his cheeks. "I never sent it," he whispered. "I was afraid she wouldn't want to see me anymore."
Anna asked him if he knew what had happened to Clara. He shook his head. "I never saw her again," he said. "But I think she was the best thing that ever happened to me."

Paul's words accompanied Anna as she left the home. She had hoped to reconnect, to bring a story to an end. But instead she had learned a lesson - about missed opportunities, about the fear that stops us from doing what we really want to do, and about the power of words to touch us even decades later.

She put the letter back in the book she had found. It was now in her apartment, a silent witness to the story she had not been able to solve completely. But she knew that the search had not been in vain. Not only had she given Paul and Clara back a piece of their story, but she had also found something within herself - the courage not to hesitate, not to wait, but to put her own words out into the world.

THE WHISPER OF THE STARS

The observatory was the only place where Jacob felt truly alive. It was situated on a hill, far from the lights of the city, and was surrounded by an endless darkness that was only broken by the stars. Night after night he sat there, alone, his eyes pressed to the telescope, while the infinity of the universe unfolded before him.

Jacob had been an astronomer for as long as he could remember. The stars had fascinated him even as a child - small points of light in a boundless expanse that promised so much and yet remained so distant. It had been his escape, his solace. In a world that he often didn't understand, the stars at least seemed honest.

But something had been different recently. It had started with an ordinary evening when he was adjusting the radio telescope, watching a band of fog and listening to the frequencies that were normally just noise. This time, however, there was something. A sound, faint, rhythmic, almost like a whisper.

At first, Jakob thought it was a malfunction, a technical problem. But the longer he listened, the more he realized that it wasn't random. It was a sequence of sounds that repeated themselves, a pattern that he couldn't interpret. It didn't sound like anything he had ever heard before - neither natural nor man-made.

Fascinated, he began to record and analyze the frequencies. For days and nights he sat in the observatory, headphones firmly on his ears, while he tried to decode the message. The whispering would not let him go. It was as if the universe itself was speaking to him, calling him, trying to tell him something.

Over time, Jakob became more and more obsessed. He hardly spoke to colleagues or friends, ate and slept only the bare minimum. His life revolved around these sounds, this whisper that touched him deep inside.

One night, when the stars were particularly clear in the sky, he heard it more clearly than ever before. The frequencies seemed to form words, strange sounds that he did not understand, but which evoked a strange warmth in him. It was as if someone was trying to comfort him, as if someone knew how lonely he was.

Jakob began to translate the sounds into patterns, symbols and numbers. He drew diagrams, filled notebooks with calculations and theories. He was convinced that the message could be decoded, that there was a meaning that would soon be revealed to him.

But the closer he seemed to get to his goal, the more he began to doubt. What if he was just imagining things? What if the whispering was nothing more than a cosmic anomaly, a coincidence that had no meaning? These thoughts tormented him, but he couldn't stop.

Finally, after weeks of work, he managed to produce a rudimentary translation. The message was fragmentary, incomplete, but it was clear: "We see you. We hear you. You are not alone."

Jacob stared at the words he had scribbled on a piece of paper. His hands were trembling. The meaning was overwhelming, and yet he felt a deep sense of calm. It was as if the loneliness that had accompanied him all his life suddenly became a little lighter.

He began to share his discovery with others, but the reactions were mixed. Some colleagues thought he was a visionary, others a crank. The world around him took little notice of his work. But that didn't matter to Jakob. He knew that the message was real, that it had changed something in him.

Night after night, he returned to the observatory, listening to the whisper that never quite disappeared. It was no longer just a sound, but a comfort, a quiet promise that the universe was not only immeasurably large, but also connected.

On one of the last nights before the observatory was to close - a victim of budget cuts and disinterest - Jacob heard something new. The whisper seemed to be saying goodbye, becoming softer and quieter, as if it knew his time here was coming to an end.

Jacob sat in the dark for a long time, his headphones on his ears, his heart heavy and yet full. The message was clear: the stars were not only whispering to him, but to all those who were willing to listen. And in this realization, he found peace.

THE CLUB OF THE IMPROBABLE

It was a Thursday, a day like any other, when nothing exciting was going to happen - and that was reason enough for Matthias to visit the old bar "Zum Loch". The name was apt, because the bar really was a hole: dim lighting, tattered sofas that looked like they had been through the Second World War and a bartender who looked like she had won it.

Matthias was 43, divorced and firmly convinced that life had deliberately dealt him the most boring version of a midlife crisis. No fast cars, no exotic trips, just him, his office job and this bar. When he opened the creaky door, he was greeted as usual by Helga, the bartender. "So, Matze, looking for meaning again?" she asked with a grin as she dragged a cloth across the bar, which was in need of a clean itself.

"Searching for meaning?" Matthias sat down on his regular stool. "I'm happy when I find a beer that doesn't taste like dishwater."

"Then you've come to the right place," Helga replied and placed a glass in front of him, the contents of which looked suspiciously like tap water. Matthias sighed, took a sip and turned around to look at the rest of the bar.

Normally the place was as empty as his fridge, but that evening he noticed something unusual: a group of people sitting around a table. They were all conspicuously unremarkable, each in their own way. A man with a stained sweater that looked as if he had pulled it out of the old clothes bin. A woman with a hairstyle that reminded of an exploded mop. And a guy with a beard so long that he could easily reach the beer on the table.

"What kind of club is that?" asked Matthias, pointing his head in their direction.

Helga grinned. "This is the club of the improbable."

Matthias raised an eyebrow. "What the hell is that supposed to be?"

"Exactly what the name says," Helga explained. "People for whom the universe provides new reasons every day why they shouldn't exist, but who carry on anyway."

Matthias laughed dryly. "So the perfect club for me."

"Actually," said Helga with a twinkle in her eye, "that's exactly what I was thinking."

Before he knew it, Helga had grabbed him by the arm and pulled him to the table. "Guys, this is Matthias. He fits in here perfectly."

The others stared at him, but not unkindly. The man in the sweater held out his hand. "Welcome. I'm Uwe. I've been struck by lightning three times and my cat hates me."

The woman with the exploded mop raised her glass. "I am Petra. I've killed eleven plants in the last five years. Recently, even a plastic cactus started to turn brown."

The bearded man nodded seriously. "My name is Thorsten. I have 17 coffee cups in my car, but not a single one at work. And I park in a no-parking zone every time without anything ever happening."

Matthias stared at her. "So that's your thing? You share stories about how ridiculous your lives are?"

Uwe shrugged his shoulders. "Well, it's better than complaining about it. If the universe doesn't take you seriously anyway, at least you can laugh about it."

Matthias hesitated, then sat down. "All right, then. I'm Matthias. My ex-wife sold our house and bought me a new coffee machine in exchange - because she thought it was a fair trade."

There was silence for a moment, then the table burst out laughing. Thorsten patted Matthias on the shoulder. "Boy, you've come to the right place."

The evening passed faster than Matthias had expected. They told each other stories that were so absurd that they almost sounded believable again. How Uwe had managed to be locked in a storage room at an airport for three hours because he had been mistaken for an applicant for a cleaning job. Or how Petra once tried to bake a birthday cake that ended up looking like a car accident - and still won prizes because people thought it was modern art.

At some point, Matthias leaned back and looked around. The beer still didn't taste good, the bar was just as run-down as before, but something had changed. For the first time in a long time, he no longer felt alone.

Later, as he stepped out into the night, feeling the rain on his face and leaving the musty smell of the bar behind him, he smiled. Maybe life was a joke that never got told properly. But in this absurd, unpredictable world, he had found something that mattered: a community of people who felt the same.

THE ANONYMOUS SELF-HELP GROUP

It was a Monday evening that felt like a Monday morning when Lisa decided to do something for her "personal development". At least that's what her best friend Claudia had called it before pushing her into the door of a windowless community center and running off with the words "It'll do you good!".

Lisa was now standing in a room that looked as if it hadn't been renovated since the 1980s. The floor was covered in linoleum-like tiles that gave off a strange smell of stale coffee and floor cleaner. A circle of metal chairs stood in the center, as if they had prepared a secret ritual - one where no one had to laugh.

"You're new, aren't you?" A middle-aged woman wearing an orange cardigan and glasses that looked like a relic from a flea market approached her. "I'm Margot. We're about to start."

"Uh, yes," Lisa stammered, trying not to let on that she wanted to run away. "I'm... Lisa."

"Welcome to the Anonymous support group," Margot said with a smile that was simultaneously reassuring and slightly creepy.

Lisa nodded, but had no idea what the group was actually for. The brochure Claudia had given her was so vague that she could expect anything from breathing exercises to spiritual group hugs.

The room gradually filled up and Lisa surveyed those present. There was a young man in a suit who looked as if he had just ruined a presentation to the CFO. Sitting next to him was an older lady nervously playing with a string of pearls . A guy in ripped jeans and a hoodie was balancing a paper cup from which a coffee-like concoction was dripping.

Finally, Margot sat down in the middle of the circle and clapped her hands. "It's good that we're all here. Before we start, I'd like to explain what this is about for the newcomers - Lisa, I'm glad you're here."

Lisa straightened up. At last she would find out why she was here.

"We are the Anonymous Self-Help Group for Chronic Embarrassment," said Margot with the conviction of a fortune teller who has just prophesied the end of the world.

Lisa blinked. "Sorry, what?"

"Chronic embarrassment," Margot repeated, as if it were the most natural thing in the world. "We've all done or said things that keep us awake at night. Things so uncomfortable we can't even confide them to our toothbrush. And we're here to talk about it."

A nervous laugh escaped Lisa before she could stop it. But when she looked around, she noticed that none of the other participants seemed the least bit irritated. On the contrary, some even nodded in agreement.

"I mean... are you serious?" Lisa asked cautiously.

Margot smiled. "Of course I will. And once you start sharing your stories, you'll see how liberating it can be."

Before Lisa could protest, the guy in the hoodie spoke up. "I'll get started. Hi, I'm Sven, and I accidentally took someone else's shopping cart at the supermarket last week. I only realized it when I was standing at the checkout trying to pay for a pack of diapers and cat food. I don't have children or a cat."

The group murmured in agreement, while Lisa wondered whether she had landed in a parallel universe.

"Thank you, Sven," said Margot. "That's a wonderful example. Embarrassing, yes, but it makes you human."

Lisa felt all eyes on her. Margot smiled at her encouragingly. "Would you like to try, Lisa?"

Lisa opened her mouth to protest, but then she thought back to the moment last week when she had accidentally written a message to her boss saying: "I read your suggestion, but to be honest, it's total garbage." She had actually meant to write to her best friend.

"Okay," she said, clearing her throat. "Hi, I'm Lisa, and I almost ruined my job last week."

A collective "Oh, we know that!" went around the room, and for the first time Lisa didn't feel completely alone. Maybe this group wasn't as crazy as she thought.

Lisa would never have thought that she would be sitting in a circle of strangers and recounting her most embarrassing moments. But here she was - and to her surprise, she didn't feel exposed, but strangely relieved. After she had told her story, the others followed suit. It was as if everyone had been waiting to reveal the worst of themselves.

The older lady with the pearl necklace - Hannelore - was next. "I accidentally passed myself off as my own daughter at a class reunion two years ago," she said, her cheeks turning pink. "I didn't want my old classmates to see how I'd aged. It got complicated when they started asking questions about 'my life'."

The room erupted in laughter and Hannelore giggled quietly as she twirled her pearl necklace. Lisa noticed how the tension in the group eased. These people were a mess - just like her.

The next person to come forward was the suit, who introduced himself as Robert. "I work in the financial sector," he began. "Last year I gave a presentation that was so important that our CEO flew in especially to see it. I was nervous and drank too much water beforehand. While I was speaking, I realized I hadn't zipped up my pants."

Collective laughter rang through the room, and even Robert couldn't help but grin. "The company boss said afterwards that I should bring more... openness into my presentation."

Sven, the hoodie wearer, spoke up again. "Guys, this is nothing. I once accidentally swiped right on my mom on Tinder. I never put my phone down that fast again."

Lisa held her stomach with laughter and Margot clapped her hands enthusiastically. "See?" she said. "Embarrassment is like glue - it holds us together. None of us are perfect, and that's what makes us special."

As the stories continued, Lisa realized that the group was more than a collection of people with bad timing. They were honest, vulnerable, and maybe a little crazy - but that made them human.

At the end of the evening, Margot stood up and smiled at the group. "Before we go, I'd like to do a little exercise. Each of you say one word that you'll take a-way with you - something that sums up today's session."

Hannelore began. "Honesty," she said in a low voice.

"Connection," Robert said, looking at everyone briefly.

"Cat food," said Sven with a broad grin.

Lisa thought for a moment before she finally said, "Acceptance."

Margot nodded with satisfaction. "Perfect. And that's exactly the point. We all carry these moments around with us, these memories that we would prefer to erase from our minds. But they make us who we are. If we accept them, we can let them go."

When Lisa went home later, she felt lighter, as if she had shed some of the burden she had been carrying around for years. She thought of the stories she had heard and the laughter that had filled the evening.

Maybe life really was a series of embarrassments - but in a world where everyone seemed to be perfect, it was comforting to know that no one really was.

And as she sank into her bed, Lisa decided that she would come back next Monday. After all, there was still plenty of embarrassment to share - and plenty to laugh about.

THE ART OF FAILURE

The workshop room was full of creative ambition and the quiet desperation that you only find in people who believe they can create "something really big". Lisa, who after the disaster with the Anonymous self-help group now thought she could discover her "buried artistic side", was skeptical before she had even set foot in the room.

The announcement had sounded so promising: "Discover the artist in you! A workshop for everyone who thinks they can't paint." Perfect for Lisa, whose only experience with art was drawing stick figures at elementary school.

The room itself seemed inviting enough: colorful paint pots, easels in a reasonably straight row, and a lecturer who looked like she'd just stumbled out of a tie-dye shirt nightmare.

"Welcome, creative souls!" shouted the lecturer, who introduced herself as Simone, with the exuberant energy of a morning person on their third espresso. "Today is not about being perfect, it's about letting go!"

"This is going to be easy," Lisa muttered as she took her seat. "I've been letting things go for years - mostly unintentionally."

The attendees around her seemed to be an interesting mix. A middle-aged man, looking too smart for the occasion, sat directly in front of her. Next to him, a woman who looked like she hadn't slept in weeks but was determined to find a muse in herself. And of course there was the guy in the beret - because every art class has to have a guy in a beret.

"Today we're painting emotions," Simone announced as she distributed the paint pots. "Forget technique, forget rules - let your soul speak!"

Lisa glanced at her blank, dazzling white canvas and felt the pressure rising inside her. Her soul seemed more in the mood for a nap than for art at the moment.

The others started enthusiastically. The woman next to her threw paint around as if the canvas was an exorcism. The man in front of her carefully painted geometric patterns that looked more like an IKEA rug than emotions. And beret guy was casting dramatic glances at his canvas before he thought he had created something "brilliant" with a single brushstroke.

Lisa, who still had no plan, decided to just pick any color. She reached for red - "Because red always looks good," she thought - and made a long, sweeping stroke. "Okay," she muttered to herself, "that's a start."

But in her nervousness, she knocked over the pot of paint, which poured over her canvas like lava. Red dripped onto the floor, and the man in front of her jumped up to save his perfectly patterned rug-in-head artwork.

"That's not letting go, that's destruction!" he shouted indignantly, while Simone applauded enthusiastically. "Yes, that's exactly what I mean! Chaos is *the core of* every emotion!"

Lisa looked at her canvas, which now looked as if she had committed murder. "That's not art," she muttered, but Simone smiled at her as if she had just discovered the next Picasso.

"Yes, yes, that's exactly it!" Simone exclaimed enthusiastically. "Look at the movement, the energy! Your emotions are literally flowing out of you!"

"Yes," Lisa said dryly, "my emotions and about half a liter of red paint."

The other participants watched her with a mixture of fascination and suspicion, and Lisa felt as if she had landed in a zoo. But somehow it was... liberating.

As she tried to put the paint pot back up, she noticed the woman next to her - the exorcism artist - looking at her head, nodding. "I like it," she said. "There's something wild about it. Uncontrolled."

"It's a bit like accident damage," Lisa muttered, but the woman just shrugged her shoulders. "Art is art."

By the time the class was over, Lisa had created what Simone called an "unorthodox" piece. Her canvas was more red than white, with a few random splashes of blue and green thrown in to give the impression that she had a plan.

But when she left the room, with a bag full of dirty brushes and a canvas that looked like it had survived the Third World War, she felt strangely content.

Lisa had not intended to go to the next workshop. After secretly depositing her 'murder scene' in a corner of her apartment, she felt sure she had learned everything there was to learn about letting go - namely that it left a mess. But when Monday came, she found herself back in the musty room with the rickety chairs.

Simone greeted the group with the same exuberant enthusiasm as last time. "Welcome back, my dears! Today we're going to go even deeper. We're not just letting go - we're surrendering to art!"

Lisa snorted softly. "Sure, I'm giving in. And the colors surrender on my shoes."

But something had changed. The group, which had seemed like a collection of strangers the first time, now felt... familiar. The man with the IKEA carpet passion - Robert, she had learned - waved to her, and the woman with the exorcism style - Martina - offered her a cup of tea. Even the guy with the beret seemed less self-absorbed as he looked halfway normal with a paintbrush in his hand.

"Today we're painting in a new way," Simone explained and pulled out a roll of wallpaper. "Collectively! Every line, every color, every idea flows into each other. No individual works, just one big piece of art."

Lisa was about to protest - collaborative sounded like an invitation for chaos - but the others were already spreading the paper out on the floor. Within minutes, the room was filled with laughter, splashes of color and random "art actions" that looked less like inspiration and more like impulsive scribbling.

"Lisa, why don't you join in?" Martina shouted as she splashed a handful of paint over the paper as if she were Jackson Pollock himself.

Lisa sighed, grabbed a paintbrush and began to paint a wobbly spiral. "If this is art, then I'm Leonardo da Vinci," she muttered, but secretly she felt more comfortable than she wanted to admit.

The hours passed and the wallpaper turned into a kaleidoscope of colors, shapes and chaos. Robert had somehow managed to include geometric patterns that went surprisingly well with Martina's anarchic splashes. Lisa continued to paint spirals that wrapped around the other elements until she realized that even the beret guy - Tom, she knew by now - had toned down his dramatic brushstrokes and worked a little more simply.

When they had finished, the group stepped back to look at their work. It was chaotic, unstructured and yet... beautiful. Each color, each line told a story that interwove with the others.

"It's art," said Simone with a broad smile. "Not perfect, but alive. Just like all of us."

Lisa stared at the paper and felt something click inside her. It wasn't a revelation, not a magical moment, but a quiet feeling of acceptance. Maybe art didn't have to be perfect. Maybe it just had to exist.

While tidying up, she helped Robert collect the paints, while Martina wondered aloud whether she could wrap her canvas as a gift - "for someone I don't like." Even Tom smiled once when Lisa handed him a paint spray gun.

As she left, Simone stopped her. "I've been watching you," she said. "You let go more today than last time."

Lisa grinned. "Yeah, I've decided that I'm just going to embrace the chaos. After all, I'm really good at creating it."

Simone laughed and pressed a small canvas into her hand. "Here, for at home. Keep the chaos flowing."

On the way home, Lisa held the blank canvas in her hand. Maybe she would paint it one day, maybe not. But one thing was certain: she had learned that art, like life itself, sometimes just had to happen.

When she looked at the first "murder scene" screen later at home, she noticed something. It no longer looked like an accident. It looked like... a beginning.

FOREVER AND NEVER

The summer they met was one of those that never seemed to end. The days were long, the evenings were bathed in golden light and the heat seemed to stretch out time. It was the year Elias saw her for the first time - Sophia, dancing with her friends in the old warehouse on the outskirts of town as if the world had been made just for this moment.

Elias was seventeen, well almost 18, in a week and still a boy in many ways. His life consisted of school, part-time jobs and the hope that something big would happen one day. The boredom of the small town had a firm grip on him, but that evening, when he stumbled by chance into this group of teenagers partying in an abandoned hall, everything changed.

Sophia was different. She had a way of laughing that sounded like a secret you were dying to know. Her eyes were dark, her movements carefree, and her voice had this warmth that attracted Elias like a flame. She was two years older, nineteen, and seemed mature in a way that intimidated and fascinated him.

It wasn't love at first sight. No, it wasn't that. It was more like a faint inkling that she could be the center of a life he couldn't even imagine.

"You're Elias, aren't you?" she asked as he leaned against the wall, trying to appear invisible. Her voice snapped him out of his thoughts.

"Yes," he said, his hands buried deep in his trouser pockets.

"I'm Sophia," she said, smiling at him. "You're not here often, are you?"

Elias shook his head. "Not really. I just... uh, stumbled into it by accident."

She laughed. "Coincidences are sometimes the best."

The conversation was brief, but it stayed with Elias. In the days that followed, he thought of her, of her smile, of the way she had looked at him, as if he was someone worth knowing.

They met again, this time in a café in the city center. It was chance - or fate, as Elias would later describe it. She was sitting in the corner with a cup of tea, a book in front of her, when he came in to get a coffee.

"Elias!" she called out and beckoned him over. He hesitated, but then sat down.

They talked about everything and nothing. About the city, which seemed too small for both of them, about music, about dreams. Sophia told him that she was going to move away after the summer, perhaps to Berlin to study art. Elias told her that he had no idea what to do with his life.

It was easy with her. Easier than he had ever expected.

Weeks passed and Elias and Sophia became inseparable. They showed each other their favorite places - Elias took her to the lake where he had swum as a child, and Sophia showed him the small roof terrace above the bookstore, which she called her secret retreat.

It wasn't just friendship, and they both knew that. It was that something you only find once in a lifetime, that feeling that the world stops spinning when the other person enters the room.

They kissed for the first time on a rainy evening, under the awning of a closed store. It was awkward and perfect, and Elias felt something shift inside him, something he never wanted to let go of.

The summer was a frenzy of long conversations, touching and the feeling that nothing could ever separate them. They talked about the future, about a life together, about all the things they still wanted to do.

But deep in Elias' heart gnawed a fear that he could not put his finger on. Sophia was like a star to him - bright, unreachable, and he feared that she might disappear one day.

As the summer drew to a close, they talked about saying goodbye for the first time. Sophia would be leaving, that was clear, but they promised each other that they would stay in touch, that they would not lose each other.
"We belong together," she said one evening as they sat by the lake, the water glistening in front of them. "No matter what happens."
Elias nodded, but there was a doubt in his mind that he couldn't express.
The summer ended, and with it began the story that would accompany Elias for the rest of his life.

Autumn came quickly, as if summer had never existed. The sun was paler, the nights colder, and the sky always seemed a little grayer. For Elias, it was as if someone had taken the colors out of the world when Sophia left. She had hugged him at the station, long and hard, and promised him that they would see each other again soon. But when the train disappeared, Elias felt as if she had taken something with her that he would never get back.

In the first few weeks, they wrote to each other every day. Messages full of longing, full of plans, full of stories from their new life. Sophia told him about Berlin - the streets that never slept, the galleries where she spent her days and the people she met. Elias, on the other hand, talked about the city that felt empty without her, about his job at the supermarket and the memories that kept catching up with him.

But as time went on, the news became less frequent. Sophia was busy, her days full of lectures and new acquaintances. Elias felt the distance between them growing, not just in kilometers, but in something deeper that he couldn't put his finger on.

One evening, when he wanted to hear her voice, he called her. She sounded tired, absent. "Elias," she said, "it's not that I don't miss you, but... there's so much going on here. Everything is so new, so different. Do you understand?"

Elias didn't understand. How could she miss him and be so distant at the same time? But he didn't say anything for fear of pushing her further away. Instead, he just nodded, even though she couldn't see it.

The weeks passed and the conversations became even shorter. Elias had the feeling that he was fighting against something invisible, a wall that was growing between them. One evening, when she didn't reply to his messages, he put his cell phone aside and stared at the ceiling of his room for a long time.
"We belong together," she had said. But now it felt as if she belonged to another world, a world to which he had no access.

The break came on a chilly November evening. Elias was sitting on the roof of the old warehouse, the place where they had first met. He had hoped that Sophia would call, that she would remember. But instead a message arrived.

"Elias, I don't know how to say this, but... I think we need to take a little time."

The words hit him like a blow. Time? What did that mean? He called her immediately, but she didn't answer. Instead, another message arrived.

"It's not your fault. It's me. I just need... space."

Room. That was the word he would hate for the next few weeks. Space was not what he wanted. He wanted her, her voice, her laughter, the warmth of her closeness. But she withdrew further and further until one day she simply disappeared.

Elias tried to understand her. Maybe she really had needed more space. Maybe it was life in Berlin that had changed her. But deep down, he knew that he had lost her.

The days turned into weeks, the weeks into months. Elias wrote to her again and again, but the replies became shorter, until at some point they stopped altogether. The silence she left behind was louder than any sound he had ever heard.

His friends told him to keep going, that things would get better. But how was he supposed to continue when the center of his world was no longer there?

One particularly cold evening, he went back to the lake where they had often sat. The wind was blowing hard across the water and the trees were bare. He sat down on the old tree trunk that had been their spot and stared at the dark water.

In his hand, he held a small note that she had given him in the summer. All it said was: "Forever."

Elias stared at the words until they blurred in his tears. Forever had been a promise they hadn't been able to keep.

But as he sat there, it wasn't just pain he felt. It was also something else - a soft, sweet sting that reminded him that they had really loved. Even though it was over now, no one could take the memories away from him.

The evening dawned and Elias remained seated while the stars rose above him. The cold bit into his skin, but he let it. It was a pain that reminded him that he had lived - and that he had loved her.

Life had a way of moving on, even if it felt like time was standing still. For Elias, the years passed like a gray fog through which he struggled. He graduated from school, took a job in the city and tried to find his way in an everyday life that felt empty and meaningless.

Sophia was still there - not physically, but in the little moments that hit him unexpectedly. Her laughter that suddenly echoed in the voices of strange women. A certain song that played on the radio and took him straight back to that summer. The smell of lavender that reminded him of the afternoon she had picked a bouquet for her mother.

He had tried to forget them. He had deleted her messages, put the memories in a mental box and tried to seal them away. But the problem with memories was that they never really disappeared. They lived on, like ghosts that couldn't let go.

He heard from her occasionally. A mutual friend once mentioned that she had opened a gallery in Berlin. Another told him that she had won an art scholarship. It seemed she had the life she had always dreamed of, and Elias was both happy for her and devastated by the thought that she had achieved all this without him.

He tried to throw himself into other relationships. There were women who liked him, who gave him affection. But every time he opened up, it felt like he was cheating on her - not the woman in front of him, but Sophia. She was the standard by which he compared everything and everyone, and no one could reach that standard.

In his heart he remained seventeen, caught up in that summer when the world was still full of possibilities and Sophia looked at him with a smile that could change everything.

Years later, when he was in his early thirties, Elias returned to the lake one evening. It was one of those nights when he felt the need to be closer to the past than to the present. The tree trunk they had often sat on was still there, but it was rotten and covered in moss.

He sat down and looked at the still water. It was still the same lake, the same place, but it felt different. Time had changed everything - except his memories.

Elias had now accepted that Sophia would not be coming back. She was part of his story, a chapter that was closed. But sometimes he wondered if she ever thought about him. Whether she ever wondered what had become of the boy who had kissed her for the first time that rainy evening.

He pulled a small notebook out of his pocket. It was full of fragments - thoughts he had collected over the years. Words that he never spoke because no one would understand them.

"You're still here," he wrote. "Not in the way I want you to be, but enough to remind me what love feels like. I wish I could tell you that I've moved on without you, but the truth is that I've learned to live with you in the past."

When he put the pen down, he felt lighter. It was a strange kind of peace - not the happiness he had once felt with her, but a kind of acceptance.

The wind carried the sounds of the night to him, and Elias remained seated until the stars faded and the first rays of sunlight illuminated the sky. It was not the ending he had hoped for, but it was an ending he could accept.

He took the notebook and placed it under a stone near the tree trunk. It was his silent farewell, a final message to the past that he could never quite let go of.

As he took the path back to the town, Elias sensed that he was no longer quite the same. The years had shaped him, changed him, but at that moment he knew that the love he had once felt for Sophia would always remain a part of him.

And maybe, he thought, that was enough.

It was a gloomy November morning when Elias saw her again. Twenty years had passed, and yet a fleeting glance was enough to throw his heart out of rhythm. He was on his way to a bookshop when he saw her crossing the street - the same springy gait he had never forgotten.

Sophia.

She was wearing a long coat, her hair was shorter, her face still had that look of vivacity that had once enchanted him. He stood still, unable to move, while she went into a café.

Elias' first reaction was to walk away. He didn't want to destroy this moment, didn't want to replace the illusion of what they had once shared with reality. But something inside him, a faint whisper from the past, made him stop.

Before he knew what he was doing, he was following her. The café was small and cozy, with a faint scent of cinnamon and freshly brewed coffee in the air. She sat at a table in the corner, leafing through a book and sipping a cup of tea.

He stood uncertainly in the doorway until she looked up. Her eyes met his and for a moment the world seemed to stand still. Then she smiled - a small, hesitant smile that bridged all the years and the distance between them.

"Elias?" Her voice was softer, deeper, but unmistakable.

He nodded, unable to speak, and walked to her table. "Hello, Sophia," he finally said, his voice brittle.

She offered him a seat and he sat down. There was silence for a moment, both of them unsure how to bridge the gap between their shared past and their separate present.

"You look good," she finally said and put the book aside.

"And you..." He paused, smiling faintly. "You too. It's been a long time."

She nodded. "Twenty years, right? And yet... it doesn't feel like that long."

At first they talked about trivial things - their work, their lives. Sophia told him that she was still active in the art scene, but now worked as a curator for a museum. Elias told her about his work in the city administration, a job that fed him but didn't fulfill him.

But eventually, as was inevitable, the conversation turned to the past.

"I've often thought about you," Elias said quietly. "Of that summer, of everything that came after."

Sophia lowered her eyes. "Me too. More than I'd like to admit. I'm sorry, Elias. I was young, and I didn't know how to..." She broke off, searching for the right words. "I didn't know how I was supposed to keep it all together."

"It wasn't your fault," he said quickly. "We were both young. And maybe it just wasn't the right time."

She looked at him, her eyes shining slightly. "Perhaps. But I regretted it. I regretted you."

The words hit him like a blow. All these years he had believed that he was the only one who had been broken by their separation. But now, in this little café, he realized that she had suffered too.

"What if?" he finally asked, the question that had accompanied him his whole life.

Sophia shook her head slowly. "I don't know. But maybe that's the point. Maybe we're not supposed to know."

They sat together for a while, talking, laughing, reminiscing. But at some point it was time to go.

As they left the café, they stopped briefly on the street. The cold of the November morning bit into their faces, but Elias felt a strange warmth.

"It was good to see you again," Sophia said, her voice soft.

"Yes," he said. "It was nice."

They hugged and then she left, her coat disappearing into the crowd like a dream that was slowly fading.

Elias stood still for a moment, then turned around and walked in the opposite direction.

It hurt, but it was a sweet pain, a reminder that he had loved and been loved.

And maybe, he thought, that was enough.

Elias didn't know how much longer he would walk the streets after saying goodbye to Sophia. The cool November air felt like a balm for the storm that was raging inside him. It was as if he had come full circle without realizing he had ever started it.

The day felt surreal, like a dream that pulled him back and forth between past and present. His head was filled with her words, her smile, the warmth of her embrace. But reality also intruded: she had left. Again.

He finally returned to his apartment, where everything was so quiet and unchanged that it seemed like a contradiction. He sat down at the small table in his kitchen and let the silence grow around him.

On the table was the old notebook that he had brought back to the lake years ago. He had picked it up again some time ago, as if he knew he would still need it. Now he opened it and read the words he had written back then:

"You're still here. Not the way I want you to be, but enough to remind me what love feels like."

These words had seemed painfully honest at the time, but now they seemed to mean something else. It was no longer just pain. It was gratitude - that he had had her, that he had been allowed to love her, even if it was only for a moment in eternity.

Elias spent the next few days in a kind of stupor. He went to work, spoke to his colleagues and completed his tasks. But in every quiet minute, he thought about Sophia. Her words, her remorse, and the fact that she had not forgotten him.

One evening, when he couldn't sleep, he took the notebook and began to write. He wrote about their reunion, about what she had said and about the questions that still haunted him. It wasn't a letter, it wasn't a message for her - it was for him. A way to process the things that had never been said.

"Maybe we could have written a different story," he wrote. "Maybe we would have stayed together, built the life we had always dreamed of. But maybe it wasn't what was meant to be. Maybe we were there to show each other what love can be, even if it doesn't last."

The words flowed out of him like a flood that had been held back for years. And when he finished, he felt lighter, as if he had let go of something that had held him captive for decades.

The next morning, he drove back to the lake. The old tree trunk was still there, although it was now little more than a pile of moss and rotten wood. Elias sat down and took the notebook out of his pocket.

He flipped through the pages, letting the words sink in one last time before slowly tearing them out and throwing them into the water. The leaves floated on the surface for a while before slowly sinking, as if swallowed up by time.

"Farewell, Sophia," he whispered, not to the woman, but to the memories he had held on to for so long.

When he stood up, he felt a strange clarity. The pain was still there, but it was no longer overwhelming. It was the sweet pain that reminded him that he had once truly loved.

Elias knew that he would never forget Sophia. But he also knew that it was time to move forward - not away from her, but with her in his heart, as a part of him that would never leave him.

The years after his reunion with Sophia passed more slowly, but they felt different. Elias continued to live, but it was no longer the mere existence that had accompanied him before. Something had changed - a quiet, steady feeling of peace that spread through him.

The sweet pain he still felt was no longer an enemy, but a companion. A reminder that love didn't have to stay forever to be significant. He carried Sophia in his heart, but she no longer determined his every decision, his every thought.

He began to spend more time with his friends, who for years had urged him in vain to come out of his shell. He discovered new hobbies - photography, walks in nature, and he even found joy in talking about stories that moved him in a small book club.

One day, when he was out and about in the city, his gaze caught on a display. It was a small second-hand bookshop filled with old, well-worn books. He entered and found himself among dusty shelves whose scent reminded him of his youth.
A woman was standing behind the counter, sorting through a pile of books. She was perhaps in her forties, with friendly eyes and a calm smile. "Can I help you?" she asked without pushing him.
"I'm just browsing," Elias replied and began to rummage through the shelves.

They didn't talk much, but later, when he brought a book to the checkout, she asked, "Do you like stories with open endings?"

Elias paused and thought about Sophia, about her story, which had never really come to an end. "Yes," he finally said. "I think I like her."

The woman introduced herself as Marie, and it was not a magical moment, not a lightning bolt that struck Elias. But it was... pleasant. Simple. Naturally.

In the weeks that followed, he returned to the antiquarian bookshop more often and they began to talk more - about books, about life, about all the little things that made up everyday life.

Marie was different from Sophia. She was quieter, less intense, but her presence had a warmth that Elias learned to appreciate. It wasn't love at first sight, but a slow blossoming, a cautious exploration of closeness.

One afternoon, while they were having tea together, Marie asked: "Do you think you can love more than once in your life?"

Elias thought for a long time before answering. "Yes," he finally said. "But it feels different every time."

She smiled, and in that moment Elias felt that he was ready to make a new start. Sophia would always be a part of him, a chapter of his story that he never wanted to forget. But that didn't mean he couldn't write any more chapters.

The love he had felt for Sophia had been great and all-consuming. The feelings he now developed for Marie were softer, calmer - a whisper that grew stronger with time.

One day, he took Marie to the lake where he had spent so many hours. They stood together on the shore and Elias told her about Sophia - not everything, but enough for her to understand why this place was important to him.

"Sometimes I think that we humans are not made to love just once," he said quietly. "Love changes, just like we change. It adapts, grows or falls behind. But it's never really gone."

Marie nodded and took his hand. "Maybe that's the point. That love doesn't have to disappear so that we can find room for new ones."

Elias looked at the still water and felt a weight lift off him. It wasn't the end, but a new beginning - not just with Marie, but with himself and the realization that love, no matter how painful or sweet, is always a gift.

And so Elias began to write a new chapter in his life - one that did not separate from the past, but embraced it as he looked to the future.

Elias sat on the old wooden bench in front of the lake. The years had marked him, his hair was gray, his movements slower, but his eyes still glowed with that light - the light of the memories and love he had experienced in his life.

Next to him lay the notebook, old and worn, but carefully preserved. It was full of the thoughts and feelings he had recorded over the years. Words for Sophia, for Marie, for himself.

Marie had died a few years ago. Her illness had come on suddenly, and although she smiled to the end, Elias had felt the world lose another piece of its warmth. But this time it had been different. The pain was deep, but he was not alone.

Sophia was still alive somewhere in the world, Elias was convinced of that. Perhaps she was still a curator, perhaps she had long since retired. They had never been in contact again, but the reunion so many years ago had healed something in him that had previously been broken.

Now, at the lake, Elias no longer felt torn. He had loved, lost, loved again and led a life that had been full of ups and downs.

He opened the notebook and leafed through the pages. The words seemed to recount a life that was so much greater than the sum of his days.

"Sophia," he whispered as he came across the old entry he had written back at the lake. "You're still here."

He smiled. It was true. She was still a part of him, just like Marie had been, just like all the people who had shaped him.

The sun began to set and the light refracted on the surface of the water, casting golden shadows across the landscape. Elias closed his eyes and took a deep breath.

"Forever and never," he murmured, the words quiet as a prayer.

As night fell, the lake remained still. The wind whispered through the trees and the stars began to shine - silent witnesses to a life full of love, loss and the sweet pain that connected the two.

And so Elias' story ended, not with a bang, but with a quiet, peaceful echo that reminded the universe that love never really disappears.

THE SPARK

In Nova Lux, the sky was always gray, an eternal veil of smoke and chemical fumes that shrouded the corporate towers like cursed monuments. The streets below were a chaos of lights, machine noise and human sweat. There were no heroes here, only survivors - and even they had a half-life.

Lina moved through the crowd, her head lowered, her hood pulled low over her face. Her fingers nervously felt the edge of the metal capsule in her pocket, as if her touch alone would prevent her from being discovered. She knew the drones were everywhere. She felt their cold eyes on the back of her neck, heard the low hum that permeated the air.

In front of her, a billboard screamed in dazzling colors: "Live better, live for us! Only 10,000 credits for the life you deserve!" The smiling man in the hologram held a cup that supposedly contained happiness. The price of happiness was high in Nova Lux, and Lina wondered how many people had sold themselves for that cup.

She ducked into a narrow alley where the shadows were deeper, where the corporations were reluctant to extend their fingers. The air smelled of rot and exhaust fumes. It wasn't better, but it was safer.

"You're late," said a voice from the darkness. A man stepped out of the shadows, his stature slender, his posture tense. Cal. His right cheek had an old scar running across his skin like lightning.

"It wasn't easy to get the thing," Lina said, her voice softer than she wanted it to be. She pulled the capsule out of her pocket and held it out to him. "Here. It's got everything on it."

Cal took the capsule and turned it between his fingers. His gaze was suspicious, but his eyes glittered with excitement. "Do you know what this means?"

Lina nodded. "Yes. And I also know what will happen if we publish it."

Cal grinned. It was a crooked, tired grin that had nothing to do with pleasure. "They'll come after us, Lina. You have no idea how far they'll go."

"Yes, you do," Lina said, her voice hard. "I know it exactly. And I'm doing it anyway."

Cal shook his head, his scar twitching. "You're crazy. But maybe that's what you need in this world."

He disappeared into the shadows again and Lina was left alone. She leaned against the cold brick wall and closed her eyes. Her thoughts wandered back - to the time before everything fell apart. To the world that hadn't been perfect, but had been alive.

It was difficult

He remembers the days before corporations controlled everything. Before every decision, every smile, every damn tear became a commodity that could be sold. Now everything was a transaction. Humanity was a cost factor that had long since been removed from the balance sheets.

"Lina!" A voice snapped her out of her thoughts. She opened her eyes and saw Nia, a girl with a tattered jacket and wide open eyes.

"They know we're here," Nia gasped. "The drones are coming. We have to get out of here."

Lina felt her muscles tense up. "How many?"

"Dozens. Maybe more."

The sounds of the marketplace had disappeared, replaced by the low, eerie hum of drones entering the alleyways. Lina took one last look in the direction of the main street, then grabbed Nia by the arm. "Come on. We need to get a head start."

They ran through the narrow alleyways, their shoes slapping against the cracked asphalt. Lina felt her coat catch on a rusty fence, but she pulled herself free and kept running. The drones were closer, their blue lights dancing on the walls.

"In here," Lina called, pulling Nia into an abandoned warehouse. The doors creaked as they closed them, and the stench of stale water filled their noses.

Nia gasped and held her side. "What now?"

Lina drew in a deep breath, her hands shaking. "We'll fight. It's the only option."

Nia looked at her, her eyes full of fear, but also with a spark that reminded Lina of herself, of the days when she had been young and naïve.

The hum of drones was everywhere now, accompanied by the march of heavy boots. They were getting closer.

Lina pulled the small explosive device out of her pocket and looked at Nia. "We have to keep the spark alive. No matter what happens."

Nia nodded. "What if we die?"

Lina snorted softly. "Then we're dying for something bigger than us."

The noises grew louder and the darkness in the warehouse was broken by blue and red lights. Lina felt the fear growing inside her, but she held it down. She couldn't give up. Not now.

"Ready?" she asked.

Nia nodded. Her hands were shaking, but there was determination on her face.

The door was pushed open and the drones rushed in. Lina raised the explosive device and whispered: "For the spark."

The first shot was fired and everything went white.

When the light disappeared, Lina only heard the buzzing in her ears. Her head was pounding and she could feel the cold concrete under her hands. Somewhere in the distance there was the crackle of fire, the screech of drones, the wail of a siren. She blinked, fighting the blurred darkness in her vision, and saw the destroyed warehouse around her.

"Nia?" Her voice was weak, a croak that barely reached above the chaos.

No answer. Lina pulled herself up, her legs trembling beneath her, and her eyes frantically searched the room. There was debris everywhere, splinters of metal and glass, and the unnaturally twisted bodies of the drones in between. The explosive device had worked.

"Nia!" she called louder this time, her voice broken.

A cough answered her and she turned around. In a corner of the hall lay Nia, her body covered in dust and blood, her hands clutching at a wound in her side.

Lina stumbled over to her, knelt down next to the girl and checked the injury. It was bad - the blood seeped through her fingers, dark and heavy.

"You need to get up," Lina said, her voice insistent, her hands frantically searching for something she could use as a bandage. "We have to get out of here before more of them come."

Nia shook her head, her eyes half-closed. "I... can't," she whispered.

"Yes, damn it!" Lina tore a piece of cloth from her coat and pressed it against the wound. "You're not going to die here, do you hear me? Not now!"

Tears streamed down Nia's face, but a faint smile flitted across her lips. "I'm sorry, Lina. I didn't mean for it to end like this."

"Stop it!" Lina grabbed her by the shoulders, her voice trembling with anger and despair. "We're fighting, remember? We won't let the spark go out."

Nia lifted a hand and placed it on Lina's cheek. Her fingers were cold, weak. "You have to keep fighting. You... are the spark."

The words hit Lina like a blow. She wanted to scream, wanted to force Nia to get up, to carry on, but she knew it was no use. Death was in Nia's eyes and he would not let her go.

"I'll be back," Lina whispered, her voice broken. She squeezed Nia's hand and stood up. "I promise you."

She turned around, her steps heavy, her gaze blank. Every step felt like she was leaving a part of herself behind.

Outside, the air was still, but the city remained loud. In the distance, Lina could hear the sirens approaching. She didn't have time to mourn. Not yet.

She pulled the hood over her head and disappeared into the shadows, her movements automatic, without thinking. She knew she had to find Cal. He was the only one who could help her secure the pod before the corporations made their next moves.

The streets were emptier than before, but she could feel the eyes of the drones looking for her everywhere. Every movement had to be precise, every breath controlled.

After hours, they reached the meeting point - a derelict factory on the outskirts of the city. Cal was already there, leaning against a broken wall, a cigarette in his hand.

"You look like shit," he said, scrutinizing her. But his tone wasn't mocking, it was full of concern.

"Nia is dead," Lina said, her voice cold and empty.

Cal paused, his face turning serious. "Damn."

"We had no choice," Lina added, sitting down on the floor. "They surprised us. There were too many of them."

"This is their game," Cal said. "They want us to lose ourselves. That we give up."

"I'm not going to give up," Lina said, her eyes hard. "But we need a new plan."

Cal nodded slowly. "We have the data. Now we need to disseminate it. We need to show what the corporations are really doing."

Lina thought of Nia, of her last words. She could feel the anger growing inside her, a flame she couldn't extinguish.

"Then we'll do it," she finally said. "For Nia. For everyone."

Cal threw the cigarette away and stood up. "This isn't going to be easy, Lina. We're going to lose more before it gets better."

"I know," she said, "but we have to keep the spark alive."

The night was quiet as they left the factory, but there was a storm in Lina's head. She knew that this was just the beginning - and that the darkness would deepen before she saw any light.

The streets of Nova Lux were a different world at night. The blinding lights of the billboards, the buzzing of the drones, the shadows of the tower giants - it all merged into an eerie, living organism. Lina and Cal moved through this chaos like ghosts, invisible and watchful.

"We need a secure connection," Cal said as they crept through an alleyway whose floor was covered in trash. "Something the corporations can't trace."

Lina snorted softly. "Are you sure? In this town? That's a bad joke."

Cal paused and glanced at her. "We don't have a choice. This data has to get out. If we don't, it's all for nothing."

Lina knew he was right. The capsule she was carrying was a key - a small but decisive blow against the corporations. It contained evidence: Documents, videos, data that showed the truth about the plundering of resources and the human rights violations of the world's most powerful companies. If they could make this information public, it would be a spark that ignited the rebellion.

"I know someone," Lina finally said. "An old contact. He works in the sewers under the districts. If anyone can get us a secure connection, it's him."

"Sewers?" Cal screwed up his face. "That sounds... pleasant."

"Welcome to the resistance," Lina muttered dryly before she started walking again.

The entrances to the Undercity were well hidden. It took them an hour to find the right one - an old, rusty trapdoor behind a disused power station. Lina knocked three times in a certain rhythm before she waited.

After a few seconds, the door opened with a creak and a man appeared. His face was marked with soot and dirt, and his clothes were nothing more than rags. But his eyes were sharp, watchful.

"Lina," he said, eyeing her, "I thought you were dead."

"Not yet, Arik," she replied, "we need your help."

Arik shook his head and stepped aside to let her in. "If you're down here, that means it's really bad."

They followed him through the winding tunnels, whose walls were covered in mold and dirt. The water flowing under their feet reeked of decay, but Lina didn't let that put her off.

"What do you need?" Arik finally asked when they reached a small chamber that he was apparently using as a workshop. The room was full of improvised technology - old monitors, cobbled-together servers, cables running through the room like veins.

"A secure connection," Cal said, "We have something the world needs to see, and we don't have much time."

Arik frowned. "You're playing with fire. If the corporations find out that I'm helping you..."

"They won't find out," Lina interrupted him. "You're the best, Arik. We need you."

For a moment he said nothing, but finally he nodded slowly. "I'll do what I can. But if you're found out, I've never heard of you."

The next few hours were a blur of sounds and flashes of light as Arik worked. Cal kept watch, his eyes constantly on the doorway, while Lina sat in an old chair and organized her thoughts.

She thought of Nia, of her last words. The spark. The thought wouldn't let her go - the belief that even the smallest hope could set off a chain of events that could change the world.

"Done," Arik finally said and straightened up. His face was even dirtier, but there was pride in his eyes. "You have a connection now. Use it wisely."

Lina and Cal stepped up to the improvised console, and Lina pulled the capsule out of her pocket. She hesitated for a moment before plugging it into the terminal. The data filled the screen, line after line, a gruesome testimony to what the corporations had hidden.

"That'll hit them," Cal muttered as he scanned over the files.

"Then let's get started," said Lina and began to upload the data.

The minutes dragged on endlessly while the progress bar slowly grew. Every noise, every shadow made them flinch. They knew that the drones would be here sooner or later.

"It's working," Arik said, but there was no relief in his voice. "But an alarm will have gone off. You have maybe ten minutes."

Lina nodded and turned to Cal. "Sure the exits. We need to be ready."

Cal disappeared, and Lina stayed behind, her eyes glued to the progress bar. 87%. 89%. 91%.

"We can do this," she muttered, more to herself than to Arik.

But as the buzzing of the drones in the distance grew louder, she knew that nothing was safe - not in Nova Lux, and certainly not in this darkness.

The buzzing of the drones grew louder, penetrating every corner of the sewers. Lina felt the vibrations through the walls, a cold tingling sensation that settled in her chest.

"Ninety-two percent," Arik muttered, his eyes fixed on the console. Sweat beaded on his forehead, even though the air was damp and cool. "It's taking too long."

Lina knew he was right. She tore off the hood of her coat to make it easier to move and reached for the small pistol in her belt. Her hands were shaking, but she forced herself to calm down.

Cal stormed back into the chamber, his breathing heavy. "They're here," he said tersely. "Three drones in the main corridor, plus at least a dozen security troops. We've got maybe five minutes."

"That's not enough," said Lina, glancing at the console. 94 percent. 95 percent. The progress bar crawled as if mocking her.

"What are we doing?" asked Arik, his face pale.

Lina straightened up, pulling her shoulders through. "We'll stop them. You stay here and finish the upload. Once it's done, encrypt the connection and delete everything. No indication that you were here."

Arik nodded slowly, his hands trembling over the keyboard. "I hope you know what you're doing."

"I hope so too," Cal muttered before following Lina.

They ran back into the narrow tunnels, their footsteps echoing on the damp floor. The hum of the drones became deafening, and soon they saw the cold blue light breaking through the corridor.

"Here," Lina said, pulling Cal into a side chamber. "We need to surprise them."

She pressed herself against the wall, her gaze fixed on the entrance. The drones floated in, three metal monsters whose lights caught every movement. Behind them marched the security troops - heavily armored figures with automatic weapons, ready to eliminate everything and everyone.

Lina waited, counting in her head. One. Two. Three.

She jumped out of her hiding place and fired at the first drone. The bullets hit the casing, sending sparks flying, but it wasn't enough to destroy it. Cal followed her example, his shots aimed at the security troops. One fell, but the others returned fire immediately.

"Get back!" Lina shouted, retreating further into the tunnel. Cal followed her, his movements frantic as the bullets struck behind them.

"This won't last long," Cal shouted as they turned a corner.

"It'll have to do," said Lina. "We have to buy Arik some time."

They reached another chamber whose ceiling looked in danger of collapsing. Lina paused, her eyes fixed on the weak metal beams.

"We'll bring them here," she said, "If we blow the ceiling, we'll block the hallway."

Cal nodded, pulling a small explosive charge from his pocket. "This is going to be close."

"When isn't it?" Lina checked her gun, her mind racing.

They heard the drones approaching, the cold light filling the tunnel. Lina aimed her gun and fired again, this time aiming at the drones' sensors. One hit - the drone crashed to the ground.

"Now!" Cal shouted and activated the explosive charge.

The explosion was deafening. The ceiling collapsed, a torrent of concrete and steel filled the tunnel, and the buzzing of the drones died away.

Silence.

Lina stood there panting, her ears ringing from the explosion. She turned to Cal, who was sitting on one knee, blood dripping from a small wound on his forehead.

"Are you okay?" she asked.

He nodded weakly. "Ask me again tomorrow."

She helped him to his feet and they made their way back to Arik's chamber.

When they arrived, they saw the progress bar. 100 percent.

"It's out," Arik said, his voice a mixture of relief and fear. "The world will see."

Lina took a deep breath. They had made it - at least this part.

But in her heart she knew that the storm had only just begun.

The success of the upload hung heavy in the air, but the relief was short-lived. The buzzing of the drones could be heard again, louder than before, and this time accompanied by muffled explosions in the distance. The corporations reacted. Quickly.

"We have to get out of here," Cal said as he pressed a hand to the bleeding wound on his forehead. "They'll search the whole sector."

"He's right," Arik agreed. "You can't stay here. And I..." He hesitated, his eyes flickering back and forth between Lina and Cal. "I'm going to have to leave."

Lina nodded. "Thank you, Arik. We couldn't have done it without you."

Arik shrugged his shoulders, but there was a hint of pride in his eyes. "Take care of yourselves. You're the targets now."

Lina and Cal shouldered their equipment and made their way through the tunnels, half-buried by the collapse of the ceiling. They moved as fast as they could, but every corner, every bend felt like a trap.

"Do you have a plan?" Cal asked, his voice tight.

"We need to get to our outpost in the north," Lina replied. "We can regroup from there. Maybe we'll have a few more allies there."

"Maybe?" Cal raised an eyebrow.

"There are no guarantees," Lina said coldly. "Not in this world."

The tunnels ended in a narrow shaft that led to an abandoned factory. Lina pushed open the rusty metal door and peered out. The factory was empty, but the sky above them flickered with the lights of the drones.

"We need to stay in the shadows," she said before stepping out.

They moved through the labyrinth of ruins, their footsteps silent, their bodies close to the walls. But the drones were everywhere, and it wasn't long before the ominous buzzing came closer again.

"Get down!" Lina hissed, pulling Cal into a dark corner. She watched as a group of drones hovered above them, their blue lights gliding over the rubble, searching.

"They know we're here," Cal whispered.

Lina nodded, her heart hammering in her chest. She reached for her weapon, but she knew that they had no chance against the superiority of the drones.

"Up ahead," Cal said suddenly, pointing to an old pipe that led into the ground. "That could take us to safety."

They crept to the opening and crawled inside. The shaft was narrow and dark, the smell of rust and mold overwhelming. But it was a hiding place - and a way out.

Minutes passed like hours as they moved through the shaft. Finally, they reached a grate that led to another abandoned factory.

"We're out," Cal said, his voice a mixture of relief and exhaustion.

But Lina knew that they were far from safe. The corporations would not rest until they had found and eliminated them both.

"We have to keep going," she said. "The outpost is still several kilometers away."

"I don't know how much longer I can keep this up," Cal muttered as he slumped against the wall.

Lina knelt down next to him and put a hand on his shoulder. "You can do this. We've already made it this far and we'll make it to the end. For Nia. For everyone we've lost."

Cal nodded slowly, but there was something in his eyes that Lina couldn't interpret - a mixture of tiredness, pain and determination.

She helped him to his feet and together they set off again. The darkness around them was thick, but somewhere in the distance Lina thought she saw a faint light - a promise she couldn't give up.

And so they fought their way on, step by step, through a world that wanted to wipe them out.

The outpost lay hidden in a dense tangle of scrap and rubble, on the edge of the Zone, where the city merged into a deserted wasteland. It was not a refuge, but a fortress of decay, guarded by people who were more afraid of the world than the drones.

Lina and Cal approached cautiously. They could make out the guards - tired faces, clad in rags, but with sharp eyes and improvised weapons. One of them raised a hand when he saw them.

"Lina?" the man called out. His voice was raspy, as if from too much smoke and too little sleep.

"Yes, Oren," Lina replied, her voice soft but firm. "It's me. We need help."

Oren eyed them for a moment before waving them through. "Come on in. But quietly. The drones have been combing the area. It's getting worse."

Inside the outpost, the atmosphere was oppressive. People sat huddled in corners, their faces marked by darkness and fear. A few of them looked up when Lina and Cal entered, but no one spoke.

"What happened?" asked Lina, looking around.

"They wiped out the settlement in the south two days ago," Oren said, lighting a cigarette. "The drones came at night, and by morning there was nothing left. We'll be next if we're not careful."

"We've uploaded the data," Lina said, her voice determined. "The world now knows what the corporations are doing. That's the first step."

Oren laughed bitterly. "The world? You mean those bloated cities full of rich bastards who don't even know we exist? Do you think they care about us?"

"You'll have to take care of it," Lina replied sharply. "We've set the spark. Now we have to keep the fire burning."

Oren looked at her for a moment, then nodded. "Maybe you're right. But that doesn't mean they won't kill us before anyone reacts."

"Then we need to be faster," Cal said, "We need to organize the resistance. There are more of us out there - we need to unite them."

Lina felt the tension growing inside her. The thought of putting more lives at risk tore her apart. But she knew that they had no other choice.

"How many people do you have here, Oren?" she asked.

"Not enough," he replied. "Maybe twenty who can fight. But most of them are exhausted, injured, or have long since given up."

"We need a plan," Lina said, sitting down at the old metal table in the middle of the room. "We have the data, and we have the proof. Now we need a way to spread the fire further."

Cal sat down opposite her while Oren remained standing, his cigarette in his hand. "The corporations will react," Cal said. "They'll do everything they can to find us and take us out. We have to be faster than them."

"That means we have to hit the core," Lina said. "The towers. Their strongholds in the city. If we hit where it hurts, we have a chance."

Oren snorted. "That's suicide."

"Maybe," Lina said, her gaze steady. "But if we do nothing, we'll die anyway."

The room was silent, only the soft crackling of the cigarette could be heard. Finally, Oren nodded slowly. "I'll help you. But if we do this, we'll go all the way."

"To the end," Lina repeated, her voice quiet but determined.

That night, they made their plan. They knew they were not heroes, but desperate people fighting in a world without hope. But in the eyes of the people around them, Lina saw something she hadn't seen for a long time: a spark.

As dawn broke, they stood ready. The darkness still lay heavy over the city, but somewhere in the distance a faint light broke through the clouds.

Lina sensed that they were on the edge of a precipice. But she also knew that they had nothing left to lose - apart from their belief in the possibility of making a difference.

The outpost lay hidden in a dense tangle of scrap and rubble, on the edge of the Zone, where the city merged into a deserted wasteland. It was not a refuge, but a fortress of decay, guarded by people who were more afraid of the world than of the drones.

Lina and Cal approached cautiously. They could make out the guards - tired faces, clad in rags, but with sharp eyes and improvised weapons. One of them raised a hand when he saw them.

"Lina?" the man called out. His voice was raspy, as if from too much smoke and too little sleep.

"Yes, Oren," Lina replied, her voice soft but firm. "It's me. We need help."

Oren eyed them for a moment before waving them through. "Come on in. But quietly. The drones have scoured the area. It's getting worse."

Inside the outpost, the atmosphere was oppressive. People sat huddled in corners, their faces marked by darkness and fear. A few of them looked up when Lina and Cal entered, but no one spoke.

"What happened?" asked Lina, looking around.

"They wiped out the settlement in the south two days ago," Oren said, lighting a cigarette. "The drones came at night, and by morning there was nothing left. We'll be next if we're not careful."

"We've uploaded the data," Lina said, her voice determined. "The world now knows what the corporations are doing. That's the first step."

Oren laughed bitterly. "The world? You mean those bloated cities full of rich bastards who don't even know we exist? Do you think they care about us?"

"You'll have to take care of it," Lina replied sharply. "We've set the spark. Now we have to keep the fire burning."

Oren looked at her for a moment, then nodded. "Maybe you're right. But that doesn't mean they won't kill us before anyone reacts."

"Then we need to be faster," Cal said, "We need to organize the resistance. There are more of us out there - we need to unite them."

Lina felt the tension growing inside her. The thought of putting more lives at risk tore her apart. But she knew that they had no other choice.

"How many people do you have here, Oren?" she asked.

"Not enough," he replied. "Maybe twenty who can fight. But most of them are exhausted, injured, or have long since given up."

"We need a plan," Lina said, sitting down at the old metal table in the middle of the room. "We have the data, and we have the proof. Now we need a way to spread the fire further."

Cal sat down opposite her while Oren remained standing, his cigarette in his hand. "The corporations will react," Cal said. "They'll do everything they can to find us and take us out. We have to be faster than them."

"That means we have to hit the core," Lina said. "The towers. Their strongholds in the city. If we hit where it hurts, we have a chance."

Oren snorted. "That's suicide."

"Maybe," Lina said, her gaze steady. "But if we don't do anything, we'll die anyway."

The room was silent, only the soft crackling of the cigarette could be heard. Finally, Oren nodded slowly. "I'll help you. But if we do this, we'll go all the way."

"To the end," Lina repeated, her voice quiet but determined.

That night, they made their plan. They knew they were not heroes, but desperate people fighting in a world without hope. But in the eyes of the people around them, Lina saw something she hadn't seen for a long time: a spark.

As dawn broke, they stood ready. The darkness still lay heavy over the city, but somewhere in the distance a faint light broke through the clouds.

Lina sensed that they were on the edge of a precipice. But she also knew that they had nothing left to lose - apart from their belief in the possibility of making a difference.

"Let's light a fire," she said quietly, before turning and stepping out into the darkness.

The city lay before them like a sleeping monster, but Lina knew that the peace was deceptive. Drones patrolled the streets, security forces lurked in the shadows, and the towers of the corporations rose into the sky like stone sentinels.

Oren had been right - the attack on the core was suicide. But suicide was a risk Lina was willing to take. Everyone in her group knew that this was no ordinary fight. It was their last stand, a desperate chance to shake the system before they themselves were swallowed up.

"The first wave is on me," Oren said quietly, checking his improvised explosive device. "I'll draw attention to myself while you get into the building."

"You won't make it," Cal said, but his voice wasn't mocking. It was a matter-of-fact statement.

Oren shrugged his shoulders. "I'm old, Lina. I've seen enough. If I'm going to die, at least it'll be for something that counts."

Lina looked him in the eye. There was nothing she could say to change his mind. She reached for his hand and squeezed it tightly. "Thank you, Oren. For everything."

Oren nodded, pulled his hood over his head and disappeared into the darkness. Lina turned to the rest of the fighters waiting in the shadows. "Be ready. As soon as the explosion goes off, we move. No hesitation, no mistakes."

Cal gave her a quick glance. "You know this is a suicide mission, right?"

"I know," Lina said calmly. "But it's all we have."

Seconds passed like hours as they waited for the signal. Finally, a deafening bang broke the silence. A pillar of fire shot into the night sky and the buzzing of the drones suddenly became louder.

"Now!" shouted Lina, and the group rushed forward, their movements quick and precise.

They reached the entrance to the tower while the security guards were distracted. Lina smashed open the security door with an improvised charge and they forced their way inside.

The corridors of the tower were cold and sterile, illuminated by bright white lights. Lina felt her heart racing, but she forced herself to remain calm.

"The server room is on the 15th floor," Cal said as they crept through the corridors. "We'll have to take the elevator."

"Too dangerous," said Lina. "We'll take the stairs."

The group began their ascent, each step a test of their endurance and determination. The hum of drones and the footsteps of security forces were everywhere, but they moved through the building like shadows.

On the 10th floor, they heard the first sound of footsteps coming towards them. Lina gave a hand signal and the group hid in an empty room.

Two security guards came by, their voices low, but Lina could hear enough. "The rebels have destroyed the outpost," one of them said. "Orders are to take no prisoners."

Lina felt her throat constrict, but she waited until the men had disappeared before continuing.

Finally, they reached the 15th floor. The server room was secured by a reinforced door, but Lina had taken precautions. She pulled a device out of her bag that Arik had given them and attached it to the door. After a few seconds, it buzzed softly and the door opened.

The room was filled with rows of servers that hummed and blinked quietly. This was the heart of the system, the fortress of the corporations.

"Go," Lina said as she walked to the main terminal. She closed the connection that Arik had set up and began to transfer the data.

Minutes passed while the group nervously kept watch. Lina could see the progress bar on the screen - 23 percent, 47 percent, 68 percent.

"Hurry up," Cal muttered, his eyes on the hallway.

Suddenly they heard footsteps approaching quickly. The security forces had found them.

"Stop them!" shouted Lina, without taking her eyes off the screen.

Cal and the others positioned themselves at the door, their improvised weapons at the ready. The first shot was fired and the building filled with noise.

Lina concentrated on the transmission, her heart hammering in her chest. 82 percent. 93 percent. 99 percent.

Finally, she heard the relieving beep that signaled the end of the transmission. The data was out.

She turned around and saw Cal and the others fighting the security forces. Blood and smoke filled the air, and Lina knew they didn't have time.

"Retreat!" she shouted, raising her voice above the noise.

Cal nodded, but his face was lined with pain. He had been hit, holding his side as he retreated.

Lina helped him while the group tried to make their way back. But the security forces were everywhere and the corridors were a battlefield.

They reached the exit, but as they stepped out, Lina saw the next wave of drones above them.

She reached for Cal's hand as the drones aimed their weapons at her. "For the spark," she whispered.

A deafening light lit up the night and it became dark around them.

When Lina regained consciousness, everything was silent. Her ears were ringing and a dull ache pulsed through her body. She blinked, trying to see the blurred world around her more clearly. Debris lay strewn about, the sky darkened by smoke and ash.

Lying next to her was Cal, his face pale and his breathing heavy and irregular. Blood seeped from the wound in his side, staining the ground beneath him dark.

"Lina..." His voice was barely more than a whisper.

"Don't talk," she said, her voice trembling as she leaned toward him. "I'm getting you out of here."

"No," Cal said, shaking his head weakly. "It's... it's over for me."

Lina shook her head, her eyes stinging with tears. "Hang in there. We've made it. The data is out."

Cal smiled weakly, his eyes half closed. "You... you were the spark, Lina. Now you're the fire."

His words hit her like a blow. She wanted to shake him, wanted to force him to stay awake, but she knew he was right. His hands went limp and a last breath escaped his lips.

Lina remained sitting next to him for a moment, her fingers clinging to his. The pain was overwhelming, a wave of despair that threatened to drown her. But she couldn't stop. Not now.

She stood up, staggering, and looked around. The drones were gone and the streets were empty. She didn't know if her group was still alive, but that didn't matter anymore. She had a mission, and she had to complete it.

She moved through the rubble, her steps slow and uncertain. The city was in ruins, the once gleaming towers of the corporations were jagged, and smoke rose from all sides.

She reached a hidden entrance to the lower levels of the city, a place she and Cal had marked as a possible retreat. As she opened the door, she heard voices - quiet, but full of life.

In the small chamber that once served as a storage room, she found survivors. People she knew and others who had joined the resistance. Their faces were marked by fear and exhaustion, but something else glowed in their eyes: hope.

"Lina!" A young woman ran to her, her hands trembling as she touched her. "We thought you were dead."

"Not yet," Lina said, her voice soft but firm.

She stepped into the center of the room, her eyes wandering over the group. "The data is out," she said. "The world now knows what the corporations have done. It's our first strike, but it won't be the last."

"What now?" a man asked, his voice brittle.

Lina looked at him, then at the others. "Now we organize ourselves. Now we fight on. For Cal, for Nia, for everyone we've lost. We won't let the spark go out."

The words echoed in the silent chamber, and Lina saw how people's shoulders tightened, how their faces changed.

They were no longer just survivors. They were fighters.

Lina knew that the road ahead of them would be full of pain and loss. But she also knew that she was no longer alone.

She was the spark that would break through the darkness. And at that moment, she sensed that the fire she had lit could no longer be extinguished.

ACCESS DENIED

It wasn't raining in New York City - the sky was too busy brooding a gray soup of exhaust fumes and particulate matter over the skyscrapers. The rain was just a rumor, just like decency and morality. There were no heroes here, only people who were too clever or too rich to get caught. And Danny "Byte" Monaghan was definitely clever. Not rich, but clever.

Danny was a hacker, but not the glorified type portrayed in movies with cool music and blue screens. No, Danny was the guy who lived in an apartment smaller than a junior manager's office and subsisted on leftover cold pizza.

His office - also known as his bedroom, living room and dining room - was a chaotic altar to technology: monitors flickered, cables lay like snakes across the floor, and a lone router buzzed like a bug fueled by too much caffeine. Danny loved the chaos. It was a reflection of his soul - or what was left of it.

That night, while the city outside was drowning in its own noise, Danny had an assignment that was a little more "heavyweight championship" and a little less "five-cent job". The request came through an encrypted channel, straight from the dark part of the internet where people paid more for discretion than they did for their taxes.

The message had been simple: "Hack into the Eden-Core system. 50,000 if you can do it. No questions asked."

EdenCore - the name alone made Danny snort. One of those super-corporations that somehow managed to save the world and exploit it at the same time. Their advertisements showed happy families and smiling scientists, but Danny knew that these people were probably working behind closed doors on things that even Dr. Frankenstein would have rejected.

"Fifty thousand?" he had muttered as he read the news. "That's either too good to be true or too good to stay alive."

But like any good hacker, Danny couldn't resist the temptation. It wasn't the money - okay, it was partly the money - but the challenge. EdenCore was a castle with a digital drawbridge, a moat of firewalls and dragons of artificial intelligence. And Danny? He was the knight who wielded a USB stick instead of a sword.

He had spent the whole day preparing, writing his programs, sharpening his algorithms. Now, at 2 a.m., he was ready. The city never slept, but its networks were slowing down - a perfect moment.

"Okay, EdenCore," he muttered, pulling on the hood of his old sweatshirt. "Show me what you've got."

His fingers flew over the keyboard as he hacked into the system. It was a cat-and-mouse game, a dance of codes and protocols, and Danny loved every damn moment of it. The first layers of defense fell easily, like butter under a hot knife. But then, deep inside the system, he came across something that gave him pause.

"What the hell is that?" he whispered as he opened the file.

It was a video, and it wasn't something EdenCore would ever show in their advertising. People in laboratories, locked up like animals, hooked up to machines that looked more like torture than science. Their screams were silent, but Danny could feel them, as if they were coming through the screen straight into his bones.

"Jesus..." He leaned back, his fingers trembling slightly.

He had uncovered many dirty secrets before, but this was different. It wasn't just illegal - it was inhuman. And now he was sitting there, a guy in a dirty apartment, with a file that could potentially ruin an entire company.

"What do I do now?" he asked himself, while the monitor stared at him like a merciless judge.

Danny had no idea that this was the moment when his life would finally be flushed down the toilet - in style, of course.

Danny stared at the screen as if he could stare at it until the decision resolved itself. The clip ran in an endless loop, the screams of people echoing in his head like a bad earworm.

"Okay, Danny," he muttered to himself as he grabbed a cold cup of coffee from his desk. "This is the kind of shit you don't want to get involved in. You're a hacker, not a fucking superhero."

But there it was again, that little rodent called conscience gnawing at him. What he had seen was bigger than any code or firewall. It was something that couldn't just be swept under the carpet.

"Damn," he cursed and pushed the cup aside.

His first idea was simple: upload anonymously, let the world see it, and then hide deep in some digital hole. But before he could put his plan into action, a buzzing sound came from his laptop.

"Oh no," Danny muttered as he identified the source. It was an encrypted call, directly from the same platform he had received the order from.

Hesitantly, he clicked on "Accept". The screen changed to a dark silhouette, its face distorted by an algorithm. The voice was deep, mechanical, and laced with just enough menace to send shivers down Danny's spine.

"Danny Monaghan," the voice began, and that alone made him wince. "We know what you've found."

"Oh, fantastic," Danny said, forcing a wry smile onto his face. "I guess you're not here to send me a thank you?"

The silhouette didn't move, but the voice hardened. "Listen to me, Danny. You have no idea what you've gotten yourself into. What you have isn't yours. It belongs to EdenCore."

"Oh, I'm sorry," Danny replied sarcastically. "I thought it belonged to the people you treat like lab rats."

"Watch what you say," the voice warned. "That's not a warning. It's an offer."

"An offer?" Danny leaned back, trying to remain calm. "Please, enlighten me."

"Delete the file. Give us your access code. And we'll forget you exist."

Danny puffed. "Sounds tempting. And what happens if I say 'no'?"

A short silence followed before the voice replied. "Then you'll see what it's like when EdenCore takes notice of someone."

"Oh, wonderful," Danny said, sarcastically slapping his hands together. "That sounds almost too good to be true. But I have a little rule: I don't work with psychopaths."

The silhouette was silent for a moment, then the voice spoke again, quieter this time, but no less menacing. "You're making a mistake, Danny. I'll see you around."

The call ended and Danny sat rigidly for a moment before finally clasping his hands over his face.

"Of course they found me," he muttered. "Why not? It's not like I had a quiet evening planned tonight."

He jumped up, pulled a few cables out of the router and began frantically securing his equipment. He knew EdenCore wasn't making empty threats. They would find him, and they would finish him off if he wasn't quicker.

As he worked, a new plan formed in his head. He would not simply delete the data - that was not an option. But he could encrypt it, copy it, store it somewhere safe. And then he had to disappear.

"Okay, Danny," he said to himself as he plugged an external hard drive into his laptop. "Time to pretend you're James Bond."

He began to transfer the data, while at the same time looking for ways to cover his digital trail. He would soon have to leave his apartment, and he couldn't be sure where he was going.

But one question lingered in his mind like a virus that could not be deleted: Why? Why had EdenCore done such a thing, and why was it so important that it remained hidden?

When the transfer was complete, Danny reached for his backpack, threw a few things into it and grabbed the hard drive.

"New York City," he muttered as he slammed the door behind him. "The city that never sleeps. Hopefully I can hide somewhere where she'll at least turn a blind eye."

He stepped out into the cool night, the hum of the city around him like the low growl of a hungry predator. Danny knew he had no idea what was coming next. But one thing was certain: it wasn't going to be a walk in Central Park.

New York City at night was a beast of its own. It had no teeth, but it bit anyway. Danny pulled his hood lower over his face as he scurried through the narrow streets of Brooklyn. Every camera, every flashing light felt like it was staring him right in the neck.

"That's a great idea, Danny," he muttered to himself. "Why not annoy the biggest corporation in the world? What could possibly go wrong?"

His feet led him to an old warehouse, one of the few places in the city where he could still find a trace of anonymity. The building was half-ruined, and the stench of oil and rust hung heavy in the air. But it was quiet, and at that moment, quiet was exactly what Danny needed.

He sat down on an overturned crate, pulled his laptop out of his backpack and started it up. He had encrypted the data and backed it up on several hard disks, but he needed to do more. EdenCore wouldn't stop looking.

"Okay, let's see what we've got," he muttered and began to search through the files again.

The videos were *the core* of the problem - and the potential solution. They showed experiments that were worse than any dystopian fantasy. Humans locked into machines as if they were not beings, but batteries. The recordings showed how EdenCore deliberately put these people in a state of complete helplessness in order to achieve "maximum efficiency".

"This one makes Frankenstein look like a hobbyist," Danny said, shaking his head.

But then he came across something new. A file that looked different from the others - more encrypted, more hidden. He cracked the code with the speed of a man who knew that every second counted.

What he found took his breath away. It wasn't another video, but a list - names, addresses, information. People who had been targeted by EdenCore. People who had possibly disappeared or would soon disappear.

"That's a bloody shopping list," Danny muttered.

His first thought was to publish the list. But then he remembered the phone call. If EdenCore reacted this way because of the videos, what would they do if he released this?

"Damn it, Danny," he cursed, slamming the laptop shut. "Why can't you just live a nice, boring life?"

He reached for his cell phone, thinking about who he could call. But the list of people he trusted was short. Too short.

Instead, he opted for a different strategy: he opened an encrypted channel and contacted someone he hadn't seen for years. "Raven," he typed. "I need help."

It took longer than expected, but finally the answer came: "You've got a lot of nerve, Byte. What do you want?"

"I've found something big. Too big to deal with a-lone."

"How big?"

"EdenCore big."

A few seconds passed before the answer came: "You know I'm not getting involved with anything like that anymore."

"You told me that last time," Danny wrote back. "But I bet this will change your mind."

There was a short pause before the message came: "Send me what you've got. But if you pull me in and it's crap, you're dead."

"Fair," Danny wrote, uploading an encrypted version of the list.

It only took a few minutes for Raven to write back. "Shit, Byte. You really are a magnet for trouble. Okay, I'm in. But we need more people."

"Do you know any?"

"I know," Raven replied. "But they won't like you. And neither will I."

"Perfect," Danny muttered and closed the laptop.

He could feel the noose tightening around his neck. EdenCore was hot on his heels, and now he had to deal with people who would probably prefer to betray him straight away.

But somewhere in his head, in the part that still believed in the irony of life, a thought germinated: perhaps this was the moment when he could not only survive, but make a difference.

"Or I'll get shot," he said to himself, zipping up his backpack.

The night was cold when he left the warehouse, but Danny could feel the adrenaline pumping through his veins. It wasn't a good feeling, but it was better than nothing.

Danny hated the Lower East Side. It had a smell - a mixture of garbage, cold rain and desperate choices. But if you wanted to meet someone like Raven, this was the place.

The meeting place was an abandoned parking garage that looked so dilapidated it caved in just thinking about building codes. Danny held his backpack tightly and counted the floors as he climbed the stairs. His footsteps echoed in the emptiness, and the silence made him more nervous than he wanted to admit.

Raven was already there. He was tall, scrawny and his clothes looked as if he had fished them out of an old clothes box. But Danny knew that the man knew more about networks and codes than anyone he had ever met. Raven was a ghost in the machine - untraceable, indestructible, and definitely untrustworthy.

"Byte," Raven said without turning around. He leaned against a pillar and smoked a cigarette, the ashes of which were dangerously close to falling onto his broken sneakers.

"Raven," Danny said, keeping his distance. "I'm glad you haven't written me off yet."

"That will come," Raven replied dryly and flicked the cigarette aside. "Show me what you've got."

Danny pulled the hard disk out of his rucksack and held it up as if it were a present that he would love to wrap up again. "This is the jackpot. Data from Eden-Core. Videos, logs, and the list."

Raven stepped closer, took the hard disk and inspected it as if he could see through the casing. "The list," he muttered. "I gave it a quick skim. These are real people, Byte. Not fantasy figures."

"Yes," Danny said. "And EdenCore wants them gone."

Raven shook her head. "This is bigger than I thought. I've organized a few people, but I'm not sure they can handle it."

"Who are these people?" Danny asked suspiciously.

"People who have no reason to like EdenCore," Raven said with a wry smile. "A couple of ex-journalists, a healthcare whistleblower, and a guy who's so paranoid he thinks the NSA is monitoring his toaster."

"Sounds like a dream team," Danny said sarcastically.

"Better than nothing," Raven countered. "And nothing is what you have without us."

Before Danny could answer, they heard the loud crunch of tires on concrete. He turned around and saw a black SUV driving up the ramp.

"Oh, great," Danny muttered. "Let me guess: Eden-Core?"

Raven shook her head. "No. They're my people. They don't come in suits and security badges."

The SUV stopped and three figures got out. The first was a woman with cropped hair and a look on her face that screamed "no bullshit". The second was a man in a shabby suit that looked like he'd bought it in the 90s and never ironed it again. The third was a guy with so many cables and devices on him that he looked like a walking server room.

"That's Claire," Raven said, pointing at the woman. "Ex-journalist. Did a story on EdenCore once and almost paid for it. The guy in the suit is Benny, the whistleblower. And the nerd in the back is Torque. He's scared of everything except zip ties."

"Nice to meet you," Danny said, raising his hand in greeting.

Claire crossed her arms and eyed him critically. "You're the guy who pissed off EdenCore? You look... smaller than I thought."

"Nice to meet you too," Danny said. "I look smaller because I'm not messing with a mega-company to fund bodybuilding."

She smiled faintly, which Danny chalked up as a small victory.

"Okay," Raven said, stepping in between them. "Stop competing with each other. We've got work to do."

They gathered around an old folding table that looked like it had been rescued from a garbage dump. Danny placed the hard disk in the middle and began to explain the situation.

"We have the videos. We have the list. EdenCore will do everything they can to get that back. What we need is a plan to make this public before they take us all out of circulation."

Torque raised his hand as if he were in school. "Uh, if we do that, they'll still hunt us down, right?"

"Yeah," Claire said before Danny could answer. "But if we get enough attention, they can't shut us all up."

"And how exactly do we do that?" asked Benny, pulling on his tie.

Raven smiled wryly. "By hitting EdenCore where it hurts. We're not just hacking their servers. We're doing it live."

"Live?" Danny asked skeptically.

"Yes," said Raven. "We stream the data. Directly to their offices, to their screens, to their networks. We make them the involuntary stars of their own show."

Danny leaned back as the idea took shape in his head. It was crazy, risky and probably deadly. But damn, it sounded like fun.

"Okay," he finally said. "When do we start?"

Raven grinned. "Now."

The room was stuffy, filled with an electric tension that burned through Danny's skin. The parking garage had been transformed into an improvised command center, with monitors, cables and generators that acted like a ticking time bomb.

"Okay, guys," Raven began, getting everyone's attention. "This isn't a drill. We have exactly one chance to publicly expose EdenCore. If we fail, we're dead. So... no mistakes."

Torque, who was still tinkering with his portable server, cocked his head. "Uh, what happens if we do everything right?"

"Then we're probably dead too," Claire said dryly, checking her notes.

"Motivating," Danny muttered and sat down at his laptop.

Raven ignored the comment. "Our goal is to stream the data live - not just to the web, but directly into EdenCore's own systems. Every branch, every office, every terminal will be flooded with these videos and the list."

"This is madness," said Benny, tugging nervously at his tie. "You know they'll find us as soon as we start this, right?"

"That's exactly why we're making it big," Raven said. "The louder we are, the harder it will be for them to shut us up without blowing their own cover."

Claire tapped on her laptop with a pen. "I have a few journalist contacts. As soon as this is live, I'll let them know. They'll pick up the story before EdenCore even realizes what's happening."

"And I've prepared a few networks," Torque added. "VPNs, proxy servers... nothing will stop them forever, but we can buy ourselves a few minutes."

Danny leaned back and looked at the group. It was like bad casting for a spy movie, but it was all they had.

"Good," Raven said. "Let's go then."

Danny grabbed the hard disk and connected it to his laptop. The data was ready, and his code was programmed to stream it. His fingers flew over the keyboard as he set up the connection.

"How does it look?" asked Claire, peering over her shoulder.

"It's on," Danny said. "Give me another minute."

Torque mumbled something to himself as he adjusted a circuit. "If this works, it's going to be epic."

"And if not?" asked Benny.

"Then that's it," Danny said dryly.

The final preparations had been made. Danny checked the progress bar on his screen once more before leaning back.

"Ready?" asked Raven.

Danny nodded. "Ready. On three."

"One... two..."

Before Raven could say "three," the lights flickered and the hum of drones pierced the air.

"Damn it!" shouted Claire. "They're here!"

Raven remained calm. "Start the stream. We'll stop them."

Danny stared at his laptop. His finger hovered over the enter key. A moment of uncertainty gripped him.

"Go on!" Claire shouted and pulled a pistol out of her jacket.

Danny pressed the button. The screen showed "Stream started" and the data began to spread.

"It's on!" shouted Danny.

But before he could breathe a sigh of relief, chaos broke out. The drones stormed in, accompanied by heavily armed security forces.

Claire opened fire while Torque desperately tried to secure his equipment. Benny ducked behind a pillar and mumbled something about "I knew this was a mistake."

Raven pulled Danny back. "We need to buy time for the stream to get everywhere!"

"How long will it take?" asked Danny as he ducked behind a concrete wall.

"Three minutes," Torque said as he tried to save a server from an impending explosion. "Maybe four, if we're lucky."

"Four minutes?" muttered Danny. "That feels like a fucking lifetime."

The next few minutes were a carnage of bullets, screams and flickering lights. Claire fought like a man possessed while Raven tried to keep the group together.

Danny held on to his laptop as if it were a lifeline. The progress bar crept forward, each pixel an eternity.

"Another 30 seconds!" shouted Torque.

But at that moment, Danny saw Claire get hit. She fell to the ground, one hand on her shoulder as she tried to keep fighting.

"Damn," he muttered, watching Raven try to reach her.

The final seconds ticked by. The progress bar reached 100 percent and a "Stream complete" appeared on the screen.

"It's out!" Danny shouted as he stood up.

But the security forces were everywhere and the drones were blocking the exit.

"We have to get out!" shouted Raven.

"How?" asked Danny, looking around.

Raven reached for a bag of explosives Torque had prepared. "Through the wall."

He activated the charge and an explosion tore a hole in the concrete wall.

"Go!" shouted Raven as he helped Claire to her feet.

The group rushed through the opening, while behind them the room burst into flames.

When they were finally outside, Danny felt the cool night air on his skin. But he knew that this was far from over.

"And now?" he asked as they ran through the dark streets.

Raven looked at him, a wry smile on his lips. "Now let's hope the world is listening."

The morning came far too quickly and far too quietly. Danny was sitting in a shabby motel room with wallpaper that looked like it had been through the last world war. His laptop hummed on the small table in front of him, and the stream's progress bar had long since disappeared. Everything was out. The data, the videos, the list - they were out, and the world could now watch if it wanted to turn a blind eye.

Raven sat on the bed, a bandage around his arm, while Torque tinkered with an improvised transmitter. Claire lay on the other bed, her shoulder bandaged, her face pale but alert. Benny had tucked himself away in the corner, desperately trying to fix a phone that had given up the ghost hours ago.

"So?" Claire finally asked, her voice brittle but full of anticipation.

"It's on," Danny said, tapping on the keyboard. "I've scoured the main channels. The video's been shared, thousands of times. It's everywhere - social media, news sites, even a few TV stations have picked it up."

"And the list?" asked Torque, without looking up from his device.

"Also out," Danny said. "I sent it anonymously to every investigative organization I could find. If Eden-Core thought they could hunt us down before we published this, they miscalculated."

"That's... good, isn't it?" asked Benny, his voice trembling.

"Maybe," Raven said and stood up. "But EdenCore won't just give up. They'll launch a counteroffensive. And I'm guessing they have more resources than we do."

"Oh, that's reassuring," Danny said sarcastically and leaned back. "So we uncovered the truth, only to be blown into tiny pieces by drones. Great."

"That was always the risk," Claire said, trying to straighten up. "But the truth had to come out. We saved lives - or at least created an opportunity to do so."

Raven nodded slowly. "The question now is: What do we do next?"

Danny stared at his laptop as if the answer was hidden inside. He knew the data was only the first step. EdenCore would mobilize their lawyers, their PR people and their security forces to cover up or destroy anything that stood in their way.

"We need a place where we're safe," Torque finally said. "A place where they can't find us."

"There are no places like this," Danny said. "Not in a world where everything is connected. If they're looking for you, they'll find you."

"Then we'll split up," Claire said, her voice determined. "We'll each go in a different direction. We'll make it harder for them to catch us all at once."

Benny looked as if he had seen a ghost. "You want me to go alone? They'll kill me!"

"They will anyway," Raven said coldly. "But if we stay together, we'll just make it easier for them."

The group fell silent as the words echoed. Danny felt a chill spread through him, but he knew Raven was right.

"What about you?" he finally asked.

"I have a couple places I can go," Raven said. "But I'm going to stay in touch. We may not be in the same place, but we're still fighting the same fight."

"This isn't a fucking revolution," Danny said. "This is an escape attempt."

"Sometimes escape is the first step to survival," Claire said.

In the evening, the group left the motel, each heading in a different direction. Claire took a bus, Torque disappeared into the crowd, Benny got into a cab, and Raven just walked off without saying a word.

Danny was left alone, with a laptop, a hard drive and an oppressive silence that almost crushed him. He knew that EdenCore wasn't far away, that they probably already knew where he was.

But for the moment - just for the moment - he felt like a person who had made a difference.

Two days later, Danny was sitting in a small internet café somewhere in Queens, surrounded by flickering neon lights and the quiet hum of outdated hardware. The café was one of the few places that still accepted cash and where the cameras were too old to be connected to EdenCore's surveillance network.

He had avoided staying in one place for more than a few hours, and this café was his last stop today. His laptop lay in front of him, the display a window to a world that was currently in turmoil.

The videos triggered a wave of outrage. News portals reported on the inhumane experiments, social media was flooded with hashtags against EdenCore, and the first protests took place in front of the company's gleaming towers.

"Check this out," Danny muttered quietly to himself as he pulled up a livestream. A group of protesters were waving signs proclaiming things like "EdenCore = Nightmare" and "Humans are not machines".

But Danny knew that this was just the beginning. EdenCore wouldn't just stand by and watch her façade crumble.

His cell phone vibrated and a coded message from Raven appeared on the screen: "They're moving. They know we're scattered and they're tracking us. Keep moving."

Danny swallowed. The game was far from over. He typed a short reply: "Got it. Any news from the others?"

Raven's reply came seconds later: "Claire is safe, Torque too. Benny... we've lost him."

"Damn," Danny muttered. Benny hadn't been the bravest, but he had been one of them.

He closed his laptop, paid for his coffee in cash and left the café. The cold wind of the city greeted him and he pulled the hood of his sweatshirt low over his face.

He walked through the streets, his thoughts a whirl of worry and anger. He had started something big, but it felt as if he had simultaneously opened an abyss that would swallow him and everyone he knew.

Suddenly he stopped. At the end of the street, in the shadow of an old building, there was a black SUV.

"Of course," Danny muttered and turned slowly.

He pulled his cell phone out of his pocket and opened an app that Raven had given him. With a few quick commands, he sent a signal - an emergency call that marked the SUV's position and was sent to Raven's network.

But he knew that wouldn't be enough. EdenCore didn't play fair, and they had more resources than he did.

He set off, walking faster, ducking into side streets and trying to disappear into the anonymous mass of the city.

His plan worked - for a while. But when he reached an empty alley, he heard the soft buzzing.

"Drones," he whispered as his heart beat faster.

He ran off, hearing the footsteps of the security forces behind him. The drones pursued him like predators, their blue lights piercing the darkness of the alley.

"Damn, damn, damn," Danny muttered, throwing himself behind a pile of old garbage cans.

A drone hovered above him, its lights scanning the area. Danny held his breath as he tried to wrestle down the panic.

He pulled out his cell phone and hacked into the drone's controls - a risky maneuver, but his only chance. Seconds later, the drone lost its balance, staggered and crashed into a wall.

The sound alerted the security forces, but it gave Danny the opportunity to leave the alley. He ran through a network of streets and alleyways until his legs burned.

Finally, he found himself in an old warehouse. The room was dark and deserted, a perfect hiding place for the moment.

He sat down on the cold concrete floor, his breath coming in gasps. He knew he couldn't run forever.

His cell phone vibrated again. A message from Raven: "We have a new lead. A whistleblower inside EdenCore wants to meet. Coordinates to follow."

Danny stared at the message. A whistleblower? This could be their last chance to overturn the situation once and for all.

He leaned his head against the wall, his thoughts whirling. The fight was far from over, but now he had a new direction.

"All right," he muttered. "One last game."

He closed his eyes as the silence of the warehouse enveloped him, preparing for the next step - whatever it would bring.

The coordinates led Danny to a disused subway system deep beneath Manhattan. It was a place that most people had long forgotten - a labyrinth of dark tunnels and rusted rails, permeated by the damp cold that only the city of eternal motion could produce.

Raven had sent the details in encrypted form. The whistleblower wanted to remain anonymous, understandably, and had agreed to give Danny information that could expose EdenCore for good.

Danny knew it could be a trap. It was too perfect, too easy. But he had no choice. If it was real, it could be the turning point they needed.

With every step deeper into the tunnels, the air seemed to get heavier. His cell phone glowed faintly, the coordinates flashed on the screen.

Finally, he reached the indicated place - a deserted platform, half-shrouded in darkness. The soft dripping of water was the only sound, apart from his own breathing.

"Danny Monaghan?" A voice sounded from the shadows, low and hesitant.

Danny turned around slowly, his hand on the inside pocket of his coat where he had hidden a small knife. "Who's asking?"

A man stepped out of the darkness. He was middle-aged, with a pale face and eyes that had seen too many nights without sleep. His clothes were simple but neat - too neat for this place.

"My name is not important," the man said. "But I have information you need."

Danny looked at him skeptically. "And why should I trust you? Maybe you're just another one of EdenCore's decoys."

The man hesitated, then pulled a small USB drive out of his pocket and held it up. "Here's some data I extracted from EdenCore's main servers . They show that the experiments you've uncovered are just the beginning."

Danny reached for the drive, but paused. "Why are you risking it? Why are you helping us?"

The man lowered his eyes. "I worked on the projects. I was a part of it. I thought I could justify it - that it was for the good of humanity. But... it's nothing but cruelty. I can't look away anymore."

Danny finally took the drive and put it in his pocket. "That's a hell of a big step for a guilty man."

The man nodded weakly. "I don't expect forgiveness. Only that you do what I couldn't."

Before Danny could say anything, he heard a familiar buzzing - the buzzing of drones.

"Damn it!" he cursed and pulled the man into cover.

"They've found us," the whistleblower said, his voice full of panic.

"No kidding," Danny hissed as he pulled out his cell phone and sent a message to Raven: "Found it. Drones are here. Help!"

The drones appeared above the platform, their blue lights piercing the darkness. They were not alone - security forces in heavy armor followed them, their footsteps echoing through the tunnels.

Danny pulled the whistleblower behind an old concrete wall. "Stay here and don't move!"

"What do you want to do?" the man asked, his voice trembling.

Danny showed his knife. "Right now? Praying they kill me first and not the drive."

The next few minutes were a chaos of light, noise and panicked breaths. Danny tried to distract the drones with improvised tricks - an old pipe he threw and a smoke bomb he made from an emergency can.

But the security forces came closer. It was only a matter of time before they found him and the whistleblower.

Just when he thought it was all over, he heard a loud roar echoing from the tunnels. An explosion shook the platform and the drones' lights flickered before they crashed.

"Raven," Danny muttered as he straightened up and looked in the direction of the explosion.

Sure enough, it was Raven who stepped out of the shadows, a shotgun in his hand and a self-satisfied smirk on his face. "Still need my babysitter, Byte?"

"You've come at just the right moment," Danny said, patting the dust off his jacket.

Raven nodded, then turned to the whistleblower. "You're the traitor? I hope for your sake that this data is real."

"They're real," the man said. "And when you publish them, the world will finally see what EdenCore really is."

"Let's go then," said Raven. "We don't have much time."

The three of them made their way deeper into the tunnels, while the buzzing of more drones grew louder behind them.

Danny knew that the fight was far from over. But for the moment, they had a new spark of hope - and that was all that mattered.

The tunnels seemed endless, a labyrinth of darkness, dirt and clammy walls that swallowed Danny and the others. The hum of the drones grew quieter, but no one dared to slow down. Raven led the group, his movements precise, as if he had traveled these paths a thousand times before.

"Where is this going?" asked Danny, his breathing heavy from the exertion.

"To an old access point," Raven replied without turning around. "We've hidden a server there - nothing big, but enough to upload and distribute the new data."

"How safe is this place?" asked the whistleblower, his voice still trembling.

Raven glanced over his shoulder. "Sure enough, if you haven't betrayed us."

The man swallowed, but said nothing.

Finally, they reached a small chamber hidden behind a rusty metal door. The room was sparsely furnished: an old table, a rickety chair and an improvised server leaning against the wall.

"That's it?" asked Danny, raising an eyebrow.

"It's all we've got," Raven replied as he locked the door behind them. "Not pretty, but effective."

Danny sat down at the table, pulled the USB stick out of his pocket and connected it to the server. "Okay, let's see what we've got here."

The data was massive. Danny could hardly believe it as he scrolled through the files. Not only did they contain more evidence of EdenCore's inhumane experiments, but also plans for future projects - including something called 'Project Genesis'.

"What the hell is this?" he muttered as he opened the plans.

The whistleblower stepped closer and pointed at the screen. "This is the next step. They don't just want to exploit humans - they want to replace them. Clones, artificial intelligence, all controlled by EdenCore."

"This is insane," Danny said as he skimmed over the details.

"Madness or not," Raven said, "it's going to happen if we don't get this out."

Danny began to upload the data while the server hummed and worked. But he felt a growing doubt in his mind.

"And what happens if we publish this?" he finally asked. "What if nobody does anything about it? What if people see it and carry on as if nothing has happened?"

Raven looked at him, his face expressionless. "Then we tried anyway. And that's more than most do."

The hum of the server grew louder as the data was transferred. Danny could see the progress bar growing - slowly but surely.

But then they heard a noise that brought their hearts to their knees. The buzzing of the drones.

"They've found us," the whistleblower said, his voice panicked.

"Of course they did," Raven growled, drawing his shotgun.

Danny looked at the progress bar. 73 percent. "We need more time."

"I'll distract her," Raven said, heading for the door.

"No," Danny said and stood up. "You can't do this alone."

Raven turned around, a wry smile on his lips. "Danny, you're the one who started this. Your job is to finish it. Mine is to make sure you get the chance."

Before Danny could say anything, Raven was outside and closed the door behind him.

The buzzing of the drones was accompanied by gunfire and explosions. Danny could hear Raven struggling, holding them back, but he knew it wouldn't be enough for long.

"Faster!" Danny muttered as he stared at the progress bar. 89 percent. 92 percent.

"What if he doesn't come back?" the whistleblower asked quietly.

"Then we'll do it without him," Danny said. "But I bet he'll be back."

The progress bar reached 100 percent. "It's out!" shouted Danny.

But the joy did not last long. The door was pushed open and security forces stormed in.

Danny jumped up, his heart pounding. "The data is out! There's nothing more you can do!"

One of the men raised his gun, but before he could fire, an explosion sounded.

Raven reappeared, bloodied but alive. "Run!" he shouted as he held the security forces at bay.

Danny and the whistleblower stormed out of the room, through the tunnels and out into the darkness.

When they finally reached the surface, Danny collapsed, gasping. "He made it," he muttered.

But when he looked around, Raven was nowhere to be seen.

The whistleblower put a hand on Danny's shoulder. "He saved us. Now it's up to us to make sure his sacrifice wasn't in vain."

Danny nodded slowly, his thoughts heavy. The fight was far from over, but for a moment he felt that at least they had achieved something.

The days that followed were a fog of anxiety, fear and loneliness. Danny was holed up in a run-down boarding house in the Bronx. The noise of the city felt alien, as if he had suddenly landed in another world.

He had taken the whistleblower to a safe place, at least as safe as it was possible to be in a world under EdenCore's watchful eye. But since then there had been radio silence. No sign of Raven. No news from Claire or Torque. Benny was dead.

Danny sat on the edge of his bed, laptop on his knees as he scrolled through the news. The videos and data had shaken the world, but the reactions were mixed.

Some didn't care. Others were angry. But the real powers that be, the governments and institutions, preferred to remain silent. EdenCore had already started to suppress reporting, sending out lawyers and PR strategists to calm the public.

"It's outside," Danny muttered to himself. "But is that enough?"

His cell phone vibrated. A coded message appeared: "Meeting point 23:00. Old print shop. Come alone. - Raven"

He stared at the message, unsure whether he should react to it. Was it really Raven? Or was it a trap?

But he knew he had no choice. If it was Raven, he had to go. And if it wasn't... well, he had reached the end of his road anyway.

The old print shop was a relic from another time. Its broken windows and collapsed walls made it a place that most people avoided. Danny entered the building slowly, his footsteps echoing on the concrete floor.

"Raven?" he called, his voice trembling.

A figure emerged from the shadows. It was indeed Raven, bloodied and with a slight limp, but alive.

"You look like death," Danny said, a wry smile on his lips.

"And you look like you're willing to negotiate with him," Raven replied dryly.

They sat down at an old table, its surface marked by years of neglect. Raven pulled a small USB stick out of his pocket and placed it in front of Danny.

"What's that?" asked Danny.

"The final nail in the coffin for EdenCore," Raven said. "The data the whistleblower had was just the tip of the iceberg. These are the original records - all the plans, all the experiments, all the names of those responsible. With this, we can bring them down."

"Why didn't you mention it earlier?" asked Danny, raising an eyebrow.

"Because I wasn't sure I'd make it this far alive," Raven said with a bitter smile. "But now it's time to knock it all out."

Danny took the USB stick and looked at it for a moment. It felt heavier than it could be, as if it was carrying the responsibility of the whole world on its shoulders.

"What now?" he finally asked.

"You take this to the net," Raven said. "And I'm out of here. Forever."

Danny nodded slowly. He knew Raven was right. But part of him wanted to protest, wanted to ask why it always had to end like this.

"Take care of yourself," Danny finally said.

Raven stood up, pulled up the hood of his cloak and stepped back into the shadows. "The same goes for you, Byte. And remember - sometimes all it takes is to light the spark."

Hours later, Danny was sitting in front of his laptop again. The USB stick was connected, the files opened up in front of him. The truth was ugly, monstrous, but it was all he had.

His fingers trembled as he started the upload. This time it wasn't just a publication. It was a disclosure to every major institution, every investigative organization, every whistleblower in the world.

He watched the progress bar grow while his heart raced. When the upload was complete, he leaned back and closed his eyes.

He knew he was a dead man now. EdenCore would find him, sooner or later. But for the moment he felt light, almost free.

The world would see what he had seen. Whether they would react to it was uncertain. But Danny had done his bit.

He sat quietly in the darkness of his small boarding house, a contented smile on his face, while the city outside continued to pulsate as if nothing had happened.

IN THE SHADOW OF FRIENDSHIP

The smoke hung heavy in the air of the small office tucked away at the back of a speakeasy. A room without windows, with a desk so old it seemed to groan under the weight of its existence. The smell of old wood, cold smoke and cheap whiskey blended into a mixture that Tony "Knox" Malone knew all too well.

Knox sat on one of the rickety chairs, his hat pulled low over his face as he waited for the man behind the desk to speak. Don Carmine Ricci was a big name in the city. A man who knew how to wield influence and who knew no mercy.

"Knox," Ricci finally began, his voice as smooth as the leather of his boots. "I have a job for you. An important one."

Knox lifted his gaze, his eyes hidden under the brim of his hat. "I'm listening."

Ricci took a puff of his cigar and let the smoke slowly escape from his nostrils. "There is someone who... lost his loyalty. Someone who thought he could do his own business behind my back."

"A traitor?" Knox asked without making a face.

Ricci nodded slowly. "Yes. And I need someone who is discreet. Someone who won't make a mistake."

Knox remained silent, waiting for Ricci to get to the point.

The don reached into a drawer and pulled out a small photo. He slid it across the desk to Knox. "That's him. Richie 'Ace' Caputo. You might know him."

Knox took the photo, his heart skipping a beat as he recognized the familiar face. Ace wasn't just an acquaintance - he was Knox's best friend. A man he'd grown up with, a man he'd roamed the streets of the

Lower East Side with before they both joined Ricci's service.

"When?" Knox asked as he looked at the photo, his voice calm even though his insides were raging.

"As soon as possible," Ricci said. "I don't want any fuss. Watch him, find the right moment, and clean it up. No tracks."

Knox nodded slowly, put the photo in his coat pocket and stood up.

"Knox," Ricci called before heading for the door.

He turned around.

"Don't disappoint me," the Don said, his voice cool as the night air over the East River.

"I won't," Knox said quietly and left the office.

Outside, on the rain-soaked streets of Little Italy, Knox lit a cigarette and let the smoke fill his lungs. His heart was beating heavily in his chest and his thoughts were racing.

He couldn't believe it. Ace. His friend, his brother in spirit. The man who had saved his life when they had gotten into a fight in a seedy bar in the Bronx.

But the rules were clear. An assignment from Ricci was non-negotiable. Either he did it, or someone else would do it - and then Knox himself would be next on the list.

"Damn world," he muttered as he expelled the smoke.

Knox knew he had no choice. But he also knew that this assignment was different. It was more than a job. It was a test.

With heavy steps, he set off into the night, ready to study his friend's habits, as he had done with all his targets. But this time another thought nagged at him: What will happen when the moment comes and he has to pull the trigger?

Knox had never had any problems shadowing anyone. It was part of his job, a skill he'd cultivated like a trade. But this time it felt different. He sat in a nondescript car, its paint job past its prime, and watched the small apartment building where Ace lived.

The streets were wet from the rain that had fallen during the night, and the lanterns cast long shadows across the sidewalk. Knox knew that Ace got up early to have breakfast at a small café nearby - a ritual he had never missed, even on the darkest of days.

"Why, Ace?" Knox muttered as he lit a cigarette. The smoke was scratchy in his throat, but he didn't care.

At seven o'clock sharp, the door to the building opened and Ace stepped out. He looked the same as always: a man with a slight grin, a worn hat and an attitude that showed he was at peace with the world - or at least pretended to be.

Knox followed him, as he had done so often, only this time with a lump in his throat. Ace went to the café, sat down at his usual place by the window and, as always, ordered a coffee and a croissant.

Knox stayed outside, leaned against a lamppost and pretended to read a newspaper. He watched as Ace read the paper, laughed and chatted with the waiter. Everything seemed so normal - so damn normal.

"How am I supposed to do that?" Knox asked himself quietly.

The days passed, and Knox got to know Ace's habits as if he hadn't already known them. He knew when he left the apartment, when he came back, where he stayed. It was routine, but it gnawed at him like a thorn that dug deeper and deeper.

One evening, when he had followed Ace to a small bar, Knox lost his patience. He entered the bar, sat down at the counter and ordered a whiskey. Ace was sitting in a corner, engrossed in a conversation with another man Knox didn't know.

He watched her, studied her gestures, looked for a clue that Ace was actually a traitor. But there was nothing. Just laughter, pats on the back and a lightness that Knox found hard to bear.

After a while, the other man left the bar and Ace was left alone, his gaze lost in his glass. Knox took a deep breath, picked up his glass and walked over to him.

"Ace," he said quietly.

Ace looked up and took a moment to recognize Knox. Then a broad grin broke across his face. "Knox! My old friend! What are you doing here?"

"I thought I'd drop by," Knox said and sat down.

They talked, drank and laughed. It was like before - two friends who could forget the world for a moment. But at the back of Knox's mind nagged the mission. Every second with Ace was another step closer to the decision he didn't want to make.

"You look tired," Ace finally said, his tone more serious.

"Long nights," Knox replied evasively.

Ace nodded, took another sip. "You know, Knox, we all have our demons. Sometimes I wonder if we can ever really run away from them."

Knox felt his throat constrict. "Maybe not," he said quietly.

The words lingered between them, heavy as the smoke in the bar. Finally, Ace said goodbye, patted Knox on the shoulder and left.

Knox stayed behind, his glass half empty, his heart heavy. He knew that he had to make a decision - and that this decision would change his life forever.

The night was quiet, but Knox's thoughts were a hurricane. He sat in his gloomy apartment, a bottle of whiskey beside him, staring at the photo of Ace that Ricci had given him. It lay on the table like evidence in a court case, and Knox was judge, jury and possibly executioner.

He had no more tears to shed. Instead, there was just this emptiness that spread through his chest, like a hole that nothing could fill.

The rain pattered against the windows, a monotonous rhythm that marked time as Knox wrestled with his inner conflict. He couldn't go to Ricci and turn down the assignment. That wasn't an option. But killing Ace? Ace, the man who'd saved him more than one night when they'd both been mere street urchins?

Knox leaned back, his gaze falling on the revolver lying on the table. A simple weapon, cold and mechanical, but heavy with the decision he had to make.

The next morning, the decision had not yet been made. But Knox knew that time was running out. Ricci had left no room for delay, and if he waited too long, suspicion would fall on himself.

He followed Ace again, this time to a small park where he often sat to look at the newspaper. Knox kept his distance, sitting on a bench and watching him.

Ace seemed calm, almost carefree, but Knox could see the shadows on his face. There was something nagging at him - perhaps Ace knew more than he was letting on.

Finally, Ace got up and left, and Knox followed him, as he had done for the last few days. But this time it was different. Ace led him to an abandoned building on the edge of town, an old warehouse that had been empty for years.

Ace entered the hall and Knox stayed behind, unsure whether he should follow him. But his curiosity got the better of him and he crept after him.

The hall was dark, only a few narrow strips of light shone through the broken windows. Ace stood in the middle, his hands in his pockets, and waited.

"You can come out, Knox," he said quietly, without turning around.

Knox stood rooted to the spot. His heart was beating so loudly that he was sure Ace could hear it.

"I know you're there," Ace continued. "I've noticed you the whole time. I knew they'd send someone, and I knew it would probably be you."

Knox stepped out of the shadows, his hand tight around the revolver in his pocket. "Ace..." he began, but his voice failed.

Ace turned slowly, his face calm but his eyes heavy with pain. "You have to do it, don't you?"

Knox nodded silently.

"Listen," Ace said, "I know what I did. I went behind Ricci's back. But I had my reasons. Things I couldn't ignore."

"What kind of things?" Knox asked, his voice brittle.

"Ricci is planning something big," Ace said. "Something that will cost many lives. I couldn't sit still and let it happen. I tried to stop it. But I knew there would be consequences."

Knox lowered the hand holding the revolver. "Why didn't you tell me?"

Ace laughed softly, without mirth. "Because I didn't want you involved. I wanted you to stay out of it. But I guess that was too much to ask."

The two men stood facing each other, their friendship like an invisible bond between them, taut and threatening to snap.

"Knox," Ace said quietly, "I know you have to do as you're told. But when you do it, do it fast. I don't want Ricci's men to catch me and do it slowly."

Knox felt his throat constrict. "Ace... I can't do this."

"Yes, you can," Ace said, his voice as calm as the rain outside. "Because if you don't, you're next."

The silence in the hall was deafening. Knox knew he had to make a decision, but every option felt like a betrayal - to Ricci, to Ace, to himself.

Finally, he pulled the revolver out of his pocket, his hands shaking. Ace nodded slightly, as if to encourage him.

"I trust you, Knox," he said.

But before Knox could pull the trigger, a loud bang sounded. Ace collapsed, a hole in his chest, while the hall was filled with the sound of echoing footsteps.

Knox whirled around and saw two of Ricci's men standing there with guns at the ready.

"The boss said you might hesitate," one of them said. "We thought we'd help you."

Anger and grief overwhelmed Knox, but he knew that this was not the place to fight. He dropped the revolver, raised his hands and stepped back.

"It's done," said the other man. "The boss will be pleased."

Knox watched as the men left the hall, leaving Ace's lifeless body behind. He knelt beside his friend, the tears finally flowing freely.

"I'm sorry," he whispered as the rain outside became heavier.

Knox knew that he couldn't save Ace - neither from Ricci nor from the decisions they had both made. But he knew one thing for sure: he would never go down the same path again.

Days passed, but for Knox it felt as if time had stood still. He couldn't get Ace's face out of his mind, the look in his eyes as he accepted the inevitable. The pain, guilt and anger inside him grew like a poisonous vine wrapped around his heart.

He had tried to carry on, had thrown himself into his work, but it was no use. Every step he took, every breath he drew, reminded him that he had lost his best friend - and that he couldn't protect him.

Knox was sitting in a small bar on the outskirts of the city, a dimly lit place where Prohibition was just a suggestion. The whiskey burned in his throat, but it did nothing to ease the pain.

"You look like shit," said a voice behind him.

Knox turned around and saw Claire, one of the waitresses who worked here. She was an old acquaintance, someone who knew when it was better not to ask questions.

"Thanks for the honesty," Knox murmured, raising his glass.

"Will you tell me what's going on?" she asked as she sat down on the bar stool next to him.

Knox shook his head. "Better not."

Claire nodded slowly, as if she heard the unspoken words. "Sometimes you have to live with the ghosts you've made for yourself."

Her words hit Knox harder than he wanted to admit. He emptied his glass and put it down hard on the counter.

"Perhaps," he said, "but sometimes those who created these spirits deserve their own reckoning."

Claire frowned, but before she could say anything, Knox got up and left the bar.

Back in his apartment, Knox sat in front of his revolver, which was lying on the table. He had cleaned the barrel, checked the chamber, every movement as mechanical as his breath.

There was no future for him. Not under Ricci, not in this city. But before he left - before he left behind the life that had destroyed him - there was something he had to do.

Ace's last words echoed in his head. "I trust you, Knox."

Knox reached for his coat, put the revolver in his inside pocket and stepped out into the night.

The club where Ricci conducted his business was brightly lit, a place full of life and noise. Knox entered through the back entrance he had used so often.

The guards saw him, nodded to him and let him pass. He was one of Ricci's confidants, someone no one questioned.

Ricci was sitting in his office, a cigar between his fingers, a glass of red wine in front of him. He looked up as Knox entered, a smile on his lips.

"Knox," he said. "Come on, sit down. I heard the job was done. Good work."

Knox stopped, his hands in the pockets of his coat. "Yes," he said. "Done."

Ricci scrutinized him, his smile widening. "I knew I could count on you."

Knox pulled out the revolver and pointed it at Ricci. The don's smile disappeared, his eyes turned cold and hard.

"What are you doing, Knox?" he asked quietly.

"This is for Ace," Knox said, his voice calm. "And for all the others you've dragged into the abyss."

Ricci leaned back, his gaze full of contempt. "You know what that means, don't you? You're not getting out of this room alive."

"Maybe," Knox said. "But at least I won't have to live with your demons anymore."

The shot was loud, echoing through the room like thunder. Ricci slumped in his chair, the glass of red wine tipped over and stained the table like blood.

Knox put the revolver away, turned and left the office. The men outside stared at him, their faces frozen in shock.

"Ricci doesn't want to be disturbed," Knox said quietly as he walked past them.

He stepped out into the cool night, the weight of the revolver still in his pocket. He knew that he would be hunted now, that there was no turning back.

But for the first time in days, he felt something he hadn't expected: peace.

The rain fell in heavy drops as Knox walked through the city streets. The lanterns cast glittering reflections on the wet pavement, and the darkness embraced him like an old enemy. Every step felt like a step into the abyss, but Knox knew he had no choice.

The news of Ricci's death would spread quickly, and it wouldn't be long before the Don's men were sent after him. But Knox was prepared - at least he thought he was.

He made his way to a warehouse at the harbor, a place where he had kept a bag of cash, forged papers and a gun for years. It was a plan B that had never really seemed real to him - until now.

The warehouse was dark and deserted, broken only by the soft sound of rain and the occasional caw of a seagull. Knox slipped inside, pulled the loose plank off a wall and reached for the bag.

He checked the contents. Everything was there: enough money to go into hiding for a while, a fake passport with a name he could barely pronounce, and an old Colt that was more for reassurance than defense.

But before he could close the bag, he heard a noise. Footsteps.

"Knox," a voice called out from the darkness.

He tensed up, pulled the revolver out of his jacket and pointed it in the direction from which the voice had come.

"Show yourself," he said quietly, his fingers tight around the trigger.

A figure stepped out of the shadows, a gun in his hand. It was Lorenzo, one of Ricci's closest men - someone who had always eyed Knox critically but never had the courage to question him openly.

"I should have known it was you," Lorenzo said, smiling coldly. "It was too clean, too fast. Ricci trusted you, and you killed him."

"He deserved it," Knox said calmly, though his heart was racing.

Lorenzo raised his gun and pointed it at Knox. "That may be. But trust is everything in our business. And you've gambled away your last one."

Knox knew that words would not save him. He reacted instinctively, throwing himself to the side and firing before Lorenzo could pull the trigger. The shot echoed through the warehouse and Lorenzo went down, a surprised expression on his face before he lay motionless.

Knox was breathing heavily, his pulse pounding in his ears. He knew that this was only the beginning.

He left the warehouse through a back exit, his bag slung over his shoulder. The harbor lay quietly before him, the ships rocking gently in the waves.

His destination was a freighter that would leave at dawn. He had enough money to bribe the captain and buy himself a passage - somewhere where the long arms of Ricci's organization could not reach him.

But even when he stepped on board the ship, Knox did not feel safe. The guilt, the burden of his decisions, was a weight he couldn't shake off.

As the ship slowly glided out of the harbor, Knox looked back at the city. The lights shimmered in the rain, a last reminder of the life he was leaving behind.

He knew that he could not return. But he also knew that there would be no real peace.

Knox sat down at the edge of the deck, lit a cigarette and looked out over the dark water.

"Ace," he murmured softly as the smoke rose into the night. "I hope you can forgive me one day."

The ocean stretched out before him, an empty, endless expanse. Knox didn't know where he was going, but he knew he couldn't stay there.

The waves crashed against the ship, a steady rhythm that put him in a state somewhere between sleep and wakefulness. And in the stillness of the night, Knox felt free for the first time in days - and completely lost at the same time.

The days on the freighter dragged on like thick syrup. Knox spent most of his time alone, keeping away from the crew and avoiding any unnecessary attention. The sailors left him alone - either because they respected his pay or, more likely, because they knew the look in his eyes. The look of a man who carried more with him than he wanted to admit.

The freighter was a rusty colossus whose engines roared constantly as it cut its way through the endless waves. Knox spent the nights on deck, his cigarette glowing in the dark, while the wind blew his hair out of his forehead.

There was something calming, almost hypnotic, about the sea. But the storm continued to rage in his head.

One night, as the stars twinkled clear above him, Knox heard footsteps behind him. He turned and saw the captain, an old, bearded man who looked as if he had seen more of the world than anyone should.

"You don't sleep much, do you?" asked the captain as he lit a pipe.

Knox shook his head. "Sleep and I haven't been friends for a while."

The captain nodded as if he understood the unspoken words. "Men like you usually have a reason to run away from sleep."

"And what kind of men am I?" Knox asked, his voice calm but with a hint of sharpness.

"The kind that leaves something behind," said the captain. "Something they can't shake off."

Knox stared at the man before looking back at the water. "Maybe. But whatever it is, it's too late to change it."

The captain drew on his pipe, the glow of the coal briefly illuminating his face. "It's only too late if you tell yourself it is. But I'm only a sailor. What do I know?"

With these words, the captain turned around and disappeared into the darkness, leaving Knox alone with his thoughts.

The freighter finally docked in a small harbor town whose name Knox didn't even register. It was a sleepy place, far from the hustle and bustle of New York - a place where a man could easily disappear.

Knox entered the town with nothing but his bag and his revolver. The streets were empty, the wind carried the smell of salt and fresh bread. It could have been peaceful, but Knox knew that peace was not in the cards for him.

He rented a room above a café, a small, sparse room with a bed, a chair and a window that looked out over the sea. It was everything he needed - or deserved.

The days passed and Knox began to blend into the anonymity of the place. He helped out in the café, kept away from the few prying eyes and only spoke when necessary.

But at night, the past returned. Ace's laughter, Ricci's cold eyes, the shot that had changed everything - they were always with him, a whisper in the darkness.

One evening, Knox was sitting on a cliff overlooking the sea. The waves crashed against the rocks, the wind tore at his clothes. In his hand he held the revolver that had caused so much pain.

"Is that all that's left?" he muttered. "A man devoured by his own demons?"

The coldness of the weapon in his hand felt familiar, almost comforting. But before he could make a decision, he looked out to sea.

The water was dark, infinite, and yet it seemed to promise something - a possibility, perhaps even a second chance.

Knox lowered the gun, his hand trembling. Maybe it wasn't too late. Maybe, like the sea, he could keep going, keep moving, even if the waves kept coming back.

He stood up, put the revolver back in his pocket and turned away. The night was still young, and the city was asleep. But somewhere, deep inside him, Knox felt a spark - a reminder that there was still something worth fighting for.

And maybe, just maybe, that spark was enough to endure the darkness.

The days in the small harbor town flowed into each other like the water that washed up on the shore. Knox had become accustomed to the routine: serving coffee in the morning, scrubbing the floors at lunchtime and sitting alone in his room in the evening. Life was quiet, almost bearable. But he knew it wouldn't last.

One afternoon, as he was sweeping the terrace of the café, a black car pulled up in front of the building. It was inconspicuous, but Knox immediately recognized that it was out of place - the shiny chrome, the sleek lines. It was a vehicle built for the streets of New York, not for this remote seaside town.

Two men got out. Both wore dark suits and hats that half hid their faces. They looked around briefly before one of them approached Knox.

"You're hard to find, Mr. Malone," the man said, his voice calm but imbued with an icy undertone.

Knox lowered the broom and his heart began to beat faster. "I think you've got me confused."

The man smiled weakly, a smile that had nothing friendly about it. "I don't think so. Mr. Ricci has many friends - and many men who will see to it that his legacy is not forgotten."

Knox felt the anger rising in him, but he held it back. "Ricci is dead. His legacy is as rotten as he is."

The man's smile disappeared. "Perhaps. But his principles live on. And we're here to make sure no one forgets what happens when someone betrays the family."

Before Knox could answer, the other man drew a gun. The sun glinted off the barrel, and Knox knew he didn't have time to think.

The first shot hit the café's wooden veranda as Knox threw himself into cover. The patrons screamed and fled as the men chased after him.

Knox stormed through the kitchen, grabbed a heavy knife lying on the worktop and ran out into the narrow streets of the town.

The pursuit was intense. The men's footsteps echoed behind him, and the shots that whistled through the air made him flinch every time.

He reached the cliffs, knife firmly in hand, and turned around. The men were close, but Knox knew he couldn't take them both out at the same time.

"You've made a mistake," he shouted as he breathed heavily. "I'm not an easy target."

One of the men laughed coldly. "We know that, Knox. That's why we're here, to do it right."

The first man charged at him, but Knox dodged and plunged the knife into his side. The man gasped and fell to the ground while his partner raised his weapon.

But before the second man could pull the trigger, Knox was already on him. He grabbed the barrel of the gun, turned it to the side and struck with all his might. The gun fell to the ground and the two men wrestled with each other, the cliffs in the background a silent witness.

Knox finally managed to push the man over the edge of the cliff. His scream echoed through the air before he fell silent.

Knox stood at the edge of the cliff, his chest rising and falling heavily. The knife fell from his hand, and he looked at the body of the first man, lying motionless in the grass.

The wind blew through his hair and for a moment he felt nothing. No guilt, no sadness - just emptiness.

He knew that this was not the end. When these men found him, others would follow.

Back in his room, Knox packed his few belongings. There was no reason to stay any longer.

When he left the city, he did not look back once.

The streets were behind him, the cliffs a fading image in Knox's mind. He was on the run again, but this time the weight felt heavier. The two men he had left behind were just a foretaste of what was to come.

The train rattled beneath him, a monotonous song accompanying his thoughts. He sat in a compartment, his hat pulled low over his face, and watched the passing landscape. Waves of fields, sleeping villages, endless forests.

"How far do you want to run, Knox?" he whispered to himself.

Days later, he found himself in a new city. Chicago. Loud, chaotic, a paradise for men who had to hide - or for those who were prepared to put everything on the line.

Knox rented a small room in a boarding house whose owners barely looked at him. He was one of many faces that came and went, a shadow among shadows.

But Knox knew that Chicago was no safe haven. Ricci's men wouldn't stop. If they found him here, they would not only take him out, but anyone who came near him.

He needed a plan - something that would end this hunt once and for all.

Knox began to observe the streets, studying the people doing business in the city's bars and backrooms. He quickly discovered that Ricci's influence in Chicago was strong. There were people who knew him and people who hated him.

One night, in a smoky bar on the outskirts of the city, Knox met a woman called Evelyn. She was a bartender, with sharp eyes and an even sharper tongue.

"You're not from around here," she said as she poured him a whiskey.

"How can you tell?" Knox asked, his tone neutral.

"You look around too much," she said, "like you're waiting for someone to come through the door."

Knox smiled weakly. "Maybe I do."

Evelyn eyed him for a moment, then leaned closer. "You're looking for trouble, aren't you?"

"No," said Knox. "But I think trouble is looking for me."

In the weeks that followed, a strange alliance developed between Knox and Evelyn. She seemed to understand the dark shadows that surrounded him without asking questions. And Knox sensed that she knew more than she was letting on.

Finally, he told her the truth. About Ricci, about Ace, about the hunt that would never end.

Evelyn listened in silence while she poured two glasses of whiskey.

"You can't walk forever," she finally said.

"I know," Knox said. "But what other choice do I have?"

Evelyn leaned back, her gaze cool. "Sometimes you have to face what's chasing you to end it."

Knox knew she was right. But what did that mean? To go back to New York? To confront the men who were hunting him?

One night, when the city was quiet, Knox made his decision. He knew Evelyn was right. If he kept running, he would never be free.

He began to make plans. Looking for contacts. To gather information. There were gaps in Ricci's organization, men who were not satisfied with his legacy.

Knox knew that he wouldn't make any friends in this business. But perhaps allies. People who had just as much to lose as he did.

Weeks later, in a basement room deep beneath the city, a small group gathered. Evelyn was there, along with a few others who were prepared to take the risk.

"We have a chance to end this," Knox said as he laid the plans on the table. "But it will be dangerous. And there will be casualties."

The faces around him were serious but determined.

"If we pull this off," Knox continued, "we can save more than just me. We can banish Ricci's shadow once and for all."

The words sounded convincing, but uncertainty remained in Knox's heart. But he knew that this was his last attempt - the last way left.

The nights in Chicago grew colder, and the streets darker. Although Ricci was dead, his influence lived on - an echo that reverberated through the men who had worked for him. Knox knew his successors would not hesitate to hunt him down. Ricci may no longer be around, but his rules and legacy were stronger than ever.

Knox and his small group of allies gathered in a basement room beneath an abandoned warehouse. The air was damp, and the smell of mold hung heavy in the room. Evelyn leaned against a wall, a cigarette between her fingers, while Frank and Charlie sat at the table waiting for Knox.

"We have an advantage," Knox began as he placed a map of the city on the table. "With Ricci out the way, his organization has fallen into chaos. But that doesn't mean we're safe. His men want to restore order - and revenge for the one who threw them off balance."

"They're not just thugs," Frank interjected. "Some of these men were loyal to Ricci to the death. They won't give up."

"That's exactly why we need to hit them before they regroup," Knox said, pointing to several marked spots on the map. "These are their most important warehouses. Weapons, money, supplies - everything they need to stay in power."

Charlie let out a low growl. "So you want to lead us against a whole mob?"

"Not against the whole mob," Knox corrected. "Just against what's left. We cut them off from their supplies. Without money, without weapons, they'll lose their control. They'll break."

Evelyn stepped forward and leaned over the map. "And how exactly are you planning this? There are four of us, Knox. You have dozens of men."

"We have to be precise," Knox said. "We strike quickly, disappear before they can react. No confrontation, no bloodbath - just targeted strikes."

Frank nodded slowly. "Sounds like a plan. But how sure are you that it will work?"

Knox looked at him, his eyes cold and determined. "I'm sure enough that we have no other choice."

The first strike was aimed at a warehouse on the outskirts of the city. According to Knox's sources, there were boxes full of cash from illegal transactions - the lifeline of the organization.

They attacked at night, when the warehouse was only guarded by a few men. Evelyn snuck through a side door while Frank and Charlie distracted the guards. Knox took the lead, a crowbar in his hand, which he used to open the lock on one of the main containers.

"That's it," Evelyn whispered when she saw the boxes with bundles of money.

"Load up as much as you can," Knox ordered. "We don't have much time."

But before they had finished, they heard the sound of engines. A car stopped in front of the warehouse and more men poured in.

"Damn," Charlie whispered. "They've found us."

Knox remained calm. "Stay focused. We'll take what we have and get out of here."

They managed to load the money onto a small truck that they had prepared in front of the door. But when they tried to escape, one of the men opened fire.

Bullets whizzed through the air, and Knox felt his heartbeat accelerate. Evelyn returned fire while Frank started the truck.

"Go!" Knox shouted, and they jumped into the car while the men continued to chase after them.

They managed to steer the car into the narrow streets of the city, where the pursuers finally lost them. But the tension lingered in the air like the smoke from their weapons.

Back at the warehouse, Knox counted the money. It was enough to seriously weaken Ricci's men - and enough to perhaps make some of them question their loyalty.

"That was close," Evelyn said as she placed her gun on the table.

"Close enough," Knox replied. "We've landed a blow. Now it's about landing the next one before they recover."

Frank looked at him, his voice calm but firm. "How long can you keep this up, Knox? How long before they find you and end it all?"

Knox was silent for a moment, then raised his eyes. "For as long as it takes. Until they understand that their time is up."

Evelyn looked at him, her gaze hard, but a hint of admiration in it. "Then we'd better start planning."

Knox knew she was right. The hunt was far from over. But at that moment, he felt something he hadn't felt in years: hope.

The wind carried the smell of smoke and oil through the streets, while Knox lurked in the shadows of the city. The previous blows had had an effect - Ricci's once mighty organization was reeling. The successors who had tried to take over were fighting over what was left. But Knox knew that one last move was needed to end the game.

"Headquarters," Evelyn said as they met in a small back room. She had a cigarette between her fingers and a map spread out on the table. "They're holed up in the old clubhouse. That's where the decisions are made."

"That's risky," Frank interjected as he scrutinized the map. "The men there are well armed. And if they know we're coming, it's over."

"That's exactly why they can't know," Knox said. "We go in, target the heads of the organization and leave a message that is unmistakable. No bloodbath - just precision."

Charlie shook his head. "It's not going to be easy. But if we pull this off, we could bring the rest of Ricci's men to their knees for good."

Evelyn looked at Knox. "Are you sure you're ready? There might not be an escape this time."

"I'm ready," Knox said, his voice calm but determined. "This has dragged on long enough."

On the night of the action, the tension was almost palpable. The old clubhouse was on a quiet street lined with dark buildings. Knox and his allies approached quietly, their movements carefully planned.

Evelyn was the first to enter the building, her footsteps as silent as a cat. She crept through the back entrance while Frank and Charlie kept watch at the front.

Knox followed her, his gun in his hand. The corridors of the clubhouse were gloomy and smelled of old smoke and spilled alcohol. Voices came from one of the rooms - loud discussions that spoke of anger and fear.

"They're already tearing themselves apart," Evelyn whispered.

Knox nodded and crept closer to the door. He glanced through the crack and saw three men shouting at each other. There were guns on the table in front of them, and a pile of money was carelessly strewn about.

"That's them," Knox said quietly. "The last remnants."

He entered, gun raised. "Hands up!"

The men froze, but one of them reflexively reached for his pistol. Knox fired and the man collapsed, while the others flinched in shock.

"Stop right there!" Knox shouted, his voice a sharp command.

Evelyn stepped in behind him, her gun also drawn. "You don't have a chance. Do what he says."

The remaining men slowly raised their hands, their faces pale with fear.

"You have two options," Knox said as he walked around the table. "You get out of this town and start over somewhere new, or you end up like your boss."

One of the men, a slight guy with trembling hands, nodded vigorously. "We're getting out of here. We swear!"

"Then do it," Knox said, lowering his gun slightly.

Evelyn gave him a look. "Don't let her think too long."

"I'll give you until tomorrow," Knox said. "After that, I don't want to hear from you again - not in this town, not anywhere else."

The men hastily gathered their things and disappeared without saying another word.

Back in their hiding place, Knox slumped heavily onto a chair. The tension fell away from him, but the tiredness remained.

"That's it?" Charlie asked as he lit a cigarette.

"That's it," Knox said. "The organization is down. They have no leader anymore, no structure. They're just shadows of what they were."

Evelyn sat down opposite him, her eyes searching his. "And what now, Knox? What are you going to do now that it's over?"

Knox thought for a moment, then shrugged his shoulders. "I don't know. Maybe I'll find a new life, maybe I'll go somewhere where nobody knows me. But I do know one thing: I'm done with this town."

Evelyn nodded slowly. "Sometimes that's all you can do. Move on."

Knox leaned back, his gaze wandering to the ceiling. The darkness of the last few months still weighed heavily on him, but at that moment he felt something he hadn't felt for a long time - a faint hope of peace.

The streets of Chicago were silent as Knox left the hideout without hurry for the first time in months. The wind carried the smell of rain and coal through the air, and the first lights of dawn glistened on the rain-soaked cobblestones.

He had no fixed direction, no clear plan. But the city that had held him in its clutches for so long suddenly seemed less threatening. Ricci's men were shattered, their power a relic of the past. Knox was free - or as free as a man in his position could be.

Evelyn was waiting at the corner of a diner, her cigarette glowing in her hand. She had told him she would go with him wherever he went, but Knox knew she was as broken as he was.

"So that's it?" she asked as he stepped up to her.

"That's it," Knox said and lit another cigarette.

They walked through the streets in silence until they arrived at a train station. Evelyn stopped, looked at him, and for a moment her mask fell.

"You're leaving, aren't you?" she asked quietly.

Knox nodded. "I have to. This town has taken too much, and there's nothing left for me here."

Evelyn looked at him for a long time, then stepped closer. "Then you'd better do it out there, Knox. Make something of this new beginning."

"And you?" he asked, his voice unusually soft.

She smiled weakly. "I'll find my way. Maybe in another city, maybe here. But whatever I do, I won't do it in the shadows anymore."

The train stood on the track, its engine roaring quietly as the passengers boarded. Knox paused, turned around again and looked at Evelyn.

"You were the best thing that happened to me in this hell," he said.

Evelyn smiled, tears glistening in her eyes. "Then get out before I change my mind."

Knox got on the train, sat in a seat by the window and looked out as the landscape slowly passed by.

The city faded behind him, and with it the memories of a time that almost destroyed him. But he knew that he would always carry the scars with him.

The train continued into the darkness, the tracks humming a soft song of freedom and new beginnings. Knox didn't know where the journey would take him, but for the first time in a long time he was ready to find out.

The train stopped at a small station in the middle of wide open country. Knox stepped out into the cool morning air, his bag over his shoulder. The silence was almost suffocating after months in the noisy streets of Chicago. Here, the only sounds were the chirping of birds and the rustling of the wind through the fields.

The town he had arrived in was little more than a village - a few houses, a general store, a church with a leaning tower. It was the perfect place to disappear, to start being who he perhaps always should have been.

Knox found a small boarding house whose owner, an elderly woman with gray hair, offered him a room for a few dollars a week. It was sparsely furnished, with a narrow bed and a window that looked out onto the fields.

"Are you here to stay?" she asked as she handed him the key.

Knox shrugged his shoulders. "Maybe. I need somewhere to think first."

She smiled and nodded. "Sometimes that's all a person needs."

In the days that followed, Knox slowly began to blend into the community. He kept a low profile, helping out at the boarding house and occasionally mending fences for local farmers.

It was a simple life, one that challenged him more than he had expected. But it was also reassuring - a distraction from the shadows that had haunted him for so long.

One evening, Knox sat on the veranda of the guest-house and watched the sun set behind the hills. The colors in the sky - orange, red, purple - reminded him of the paintings his mother used to admire.

Evelyn's words echoed in his head: "Make something of this new beginning."

Knox reached for a small notebook he had found in his pocket and began to write. There were no great thoughts, no poetic sentences - just fragments, memories, things that tormented him.

Writing became a routine, a kind of therapy. Little by little, he found words for what had haunted him for so long.

Weeks passed, then months. Knox became an integral part of the small community. People respected him, even though they didn't know much about him. They sensed that he was someone who had run away from something, but they didn't ask.

One day, while he was helping to load a cart at the market, a young woman approached him. She was new in town, a teacher who had just started teaching the children of the community.

"I've heard you're the man for everything," she said with a smile.

Knox nodded. "That's what they say. What do you need?"

"A door that's stuck," she said, "could you take a look?"

He followed her to her small house and repaired the door in a few minutes. But something new began that day - a friendship, perhaps even more.

Knox knew that he could never completely shake off the past. But at this moment, in this city, he felt alive.

It wasn't a perfect life, but it was his - and that was more than he had ever dared to hope for.

The months in the small town passed quickly and Knox began to get used to the quiet life. But even in the silence, he did not find complete peace. The past was a constant companion, a shadow that lurked in the corners of his mind.

The young teacher, whose name was Anna, had become a constant in his life. Their conversations, often during a walk through the fields or a dinner on her porch, were a kind of refuge for Knox. She asked no questions about his past and seemed content with the present.

But one evening, while they were looking at the stars together, Anna said what Knox had always feared.

"Knox," she began softly, "you're carrying something inside you that won't let go. Something heavy."

Knox stared into the darkness. "Maybe," he muttered.

"Sometimes it helps to talk about it," she said, "not to solve it, but to share it."

Knox was silent for a long time. Finally, he shook his head. "Some things are better left where they are - buried."

The days following this conversation were characterized by a quiet tension. Anna dropped the subject, but Knox could sense her concern.

One afternoon, while he was repairing fences for one of the farmers, a strange wagon stopped on the dirt road. Knox froze when he saw the men in the wagon. Two faces he knew from another time - from another life.

They got out, their movements calm but menacing. "Knox," said the taller of the two, a man called Vito, who had once been one of Ricci's henchmen.

"What are you doing here?" asked Knox, without interrupting his work.

"You thought you could just disappear?" Vito said with a smile that had no warmth. "Ricci may be dead, but there are still people who haven't forgotten you."

"I'm done with this life," Knox said, setting the hammer aside.

"That may be," Vito replied, "but life hasn't finished with you."

The men asked Knox to come with them. They said they had a new boss, someone who knew how to settle old scores.

Knox knew he had no choice. If he didn't go, the village - and Anna - would be drawn into the maelstrom of his past.

The journey took him to an abandoned factory on the outskirts of the city, where the air smelled of rust and oil. The new boss was waiting there, a man called Salvatore, who had taken over Ricci's power.

"Knox," Salvatore said when he saw him. "You're a legend. The man who killed Ricci and disappeared."

"What do you want from me?" Knox asked as he surveyed his surroundings.

"There are things that still need to be done," said Salvatore. "And you will get them done."

"I'm out," Knox said, his voice firm.

Salvatore laughed softly. "No one is ever really out, Knox. You can help us - or we can destroy what you've built up in this little nest."

Back in his room at the boarding house, Knox sat in the dark for a long time. The old revolver lay on the table in front of him, a silent witness to his inner struggles.

He knew that he was being drawn back into the life he wanted to leave behind. But something was different this time. This time there were people he had to protect.

With a deep breath, Knox stood up, tucked the revolver into his jacket and stepped out into the cool night.

"If they want to play a game," he muttered, "I'll play along."

Knox knew that his plan would mean all or nothing. There was no margin for error, no do-over. Salvatore was not only a dangerous man, but also a paranoid who distrusted everyone - even his closest confidants. But that was precisely Knox's advantage.

He spent days watching Salvatore's men, studying their movements and finding their weak spots. Evelyn had helped him circulate false information that lured some of Salvatore's key men out of the city. It was a risky game, but it worked.

The time had come. A cold, clear night, the city lay silent under a dark sky. Knox prepared himself in his small guesthouse, checked his weapon and the knife he had hidden in his boot.

The old clubhouse where Salvatore was holed up was dimly lit. Knox knew the guards were reduced - most of the men were on other missions, as he had planned.

Knox crept through the back of the building, where a barred window allowed a view into the cellar. There he saw Salvatore, surrounded by just two men sitting at a table playing cards.

"This is my chance," Knox whispered to himself.

He quietly broke the lock on the back door and moved through the narrow corridors of the building. The footsteps of the men in the basement echoed softly, but Knox went unnoticed.

When he reached the cellar, he drew his gun and pointed it at the two men before they could react.

"Get down on the floor," he ordered.

They hesitated, but when they saw the look in his eyes, they obeyed.

Salvatore sat quietly, his hands on the table, and looked at Knox with a narrow smile. "Knox. I was hoping you'd come."

"Then you won't be surprised how this ends," Knox replied as he pointed the gun at him.

"You've changed," Salvatore said as he stood up. "You were one of us. Now you think you can fight the system? Against me?"

"The system is broken," Knox said. "And you're just another part of it."

Salvatore laughed coldly. "Perhaps. But you're just like me. A survivor."

Before Knox could react, Salvatore knocked over the table and reached for a gun hidden under the top. The shots echoed through the cellar and Knox jumped to the side as a bullet flew just past his head.

The two men on the ground took the opportunity to attack, but Knox was quicker. With a well-aimed shot and a slash with his knife, he put them out of action.

Salvatore used the moment to flee into an adjoining room. Knox followed him, his breathing heavy but his determination unbroken.

The room was small, little more than a storeroom, but Salvatore had created one last defense . He held a shotgun, his gaze cold and calculating.

"This is it, Knox," Salvatore said. "The moment of truth. Which one of us is going to walk out of here alive?"

Knox pointed his gun at him, his hands steady. "I have nothing left to lose, Salvatore. You do."

Salvatore laughed bitterly. "That's what makes us different. I always have something to lose. And that makes me more dangerous."

The shots were fired almost simultaneously. Salvatore was thrown back, his shotgun fell clattering to the ground. Knox felt the pain in his shoulder where a bullet had grazed him, but he remained standing.

Salvatore lay motionless on the floor, blood slowly seeping from his chest. Knox stood over him, the gun still in his hand.

"It's over," he said quietly.

Back at his boarding house, Knox cleaned the wound on his shoulder and looked out of the window at the city. The streets were quiet, as always, but there was a strange calm inside him.

Anna stepped into the room, her eyes full of worry. "What happened?"

Knox looked at her, a faint smile on his lips. "I finished something I should have finished a long time ago."

Anna sat down next to him and took his hand. "And now?"

Knox looked out again, the first rays of the morning sun illuminating the horizon. "Now? Now I'm starting to live."

The world had left Knox with many scars, but that morning he felt lighter. The past was not forgotten, but it had lost its grip on him.

The sun rose slowly over the horizon as Knox walked through the small town along the narrow main street. The sky was bathed in warm colors, and the cool morning air was filled with the buzzing of insects and the distant sound of cowbells. It was the first time in years that Knox had looked at the world without the pressure of fear or the weight of his past.

Anna was waiting outside the café, a cup of coffee in her hand. She smiled when she saw Knox approaching.

"You look like you've actually been asleep," she said teasingly.

Knox shrugged his shoulders. "Maybe I have, too. For the first time in ages."

She handed him a cup and they sat down at one of the small tables on the terrace. The street in front of them was quiet and the world felt infinitely far away.

"So, what are you going to do now?" Anna finally asked, her voice quiet but curious.

Knox thought for a moment before answering. "I don't know. Maybe I'll stay here. Maybe I'll look for something new. But whatever I do, I don't want to look back."

Anna nodded slowly. "That's a good start."

They drank their coffee in silent agreement as the city slowly awoke. It was a simple moment, but for Knox it felt like a milestone - a step in a direction he had never thought possible.

The next few weeks were an interplay of work and quiet evenings with Anna. The community began to see Knox as one of them, and for the first time he didn't feel like an outsider.

Evelyn sent him a message one day - a simple telegram with the words: **"Stay clean. Evelyn. "**

Knox smiled as he read the news. Evelyn had helped him bring about the end of Salvatore's empire, and now she seemed to have found a new beginning as well.

One afternoon, while Knox was repairing the old fences on the edge of town, a car stopped on the dusty road. It wasn't a luxurious car, just an old model with worn tires. A man got out whose face looked vaguely familiar to Knox.

"They're hard to find," the man said as he approached.

Knox put the hammer aside and straightened up. "Who's asking?"

The man pulled a cigarette out of his pocket and lit it. "Just call me Malone. I've heard you're someone who knows his way around difficult situations."

Knox frowned. "I'm through with these things."

Malone smiled faintly. "That's what they all say. Until someone comes along who really needs their skills."

Knox thought for a moment, his thoughts whirling. But then he shook his head. "Not this time."

Malone nodded as if he had been expecting the answer. He turned and got into his car. "If you change your mind," he said before closing the door, "you know where to find me."

As the car disappeared in a cloud of dust, Knox was left alone, the landscape stretching wide and open before him. He felt the temptation, the challenge, but he knew that he had chosen a different life - one that did not live in the shadows.

He grabbed the hammer and returned to his work, a slight smile on his lips.

The past was a part of him, but it was no longer what defined him.